SUPER FETUS

ADAM PEPPER

Eraserhead Press
Portland, OR

ERASERHEAD PRESS
205 NE BRYANT
PORTLAND, OR 97211

WWW.ERASERHEADPRESS.COM

ISBN: 1-933929-88-X

ACKNOWLEDGEMENTS

Super Fetus began as a whacky short that was meant to entertain a rowdy crowd at The World Horror Convention in Chicago in 2002. I hoped people would get a kick out of it but I had no idea it would take on a life of its own. I want to thank Brian Keene for publishing the original short story in the old Horrorfind Webzine. Also for their encouragement and for simply letting me know they enjoyed my story, thanks to John Everson, Rebecca Clarke, John Turi, Carlton Mellick, Kelly Laymon, Dallas Mayr, Doug Clegg and especially Rose Solar, my first fan (other than my mother). And special thanks to Rose O'Keefe at Eraserhead Press for working with me tirelessly until we got it right.

AUTHOR'S NOTE

This is not intended as a social statement. People read this story and often ask me if this is an anti-abortion piece. It is not. Others ask me if this is supposed to be a satirical pro-choice piece. Nope. No political agenda here, friends. Others have told me this story offends and upsets them. I can accept that, but I didn't write this story simply to offend. I wrote this story because I thought it was good wholesome American fun and because it occurred to me that there simply aren't enough positive role models for our young, developing fetuses today.

Enjoy!

A.P.

ONE

∂

I think mommy wants me out of here. She keeps muttering, whining, bitching and moaning. Complain, complain, complain—like a two-year-old—to any poor sap who'll listen.

"My feet hurt!" *I hear her say. I can feel her squat while trying vainly to rub her swollen toes.* "God! How am I gonna squeeze those humongous things into my shoes."

Oh, please, Mother. Get over it.

"My stomach hurts!" *she groans while rubbing her aching belly and belching like a truck driver after downing a six of Old Milwaukee.* "My waist used to be twenty-five inches."

Yeah, okay, Mommy. When you were like fourteen, maybe.

"My ass is fat!" *she whines while pinching the ripples of her own ass with her bloated thumb and forefinger, then shaking the unsightly flab up and down, as if that'll somehow magically make her blubber-packed bottom shrink.* "If this wedgee goes any further up my butt, I am going to freak. It's disgusting! And I am not getting into those giant maternity underwears."

All she does is complain!

"I have to pee again," *she sighs, then scampers to the bathroom, squeezing her insides together so as not to have an accident. I can feel her thighs squinching together to the point that I'm getting a serious headache.*

"I'm hungry again," *she says at least five times a day, then raids the fridge of anything and everything, depending*

7

on the craving of the moment; could be ice cream, could be sardines; could be pickles, could be grape jam. Sometimes it's none of the above. Other times it's all of the above, slapped onto a potato roll and devoured in four bites, tops. Which is followed by the inevitable lament, "I ate too much again." And then, of course, the ensuing tummy rubs, more belching, and more farting. She's such a lady, my mom. She's so dainty.

Wah. Wah. Wah. Bitch. Bitch. Bitch. Moan. Whine. Complain. Over and over and over again. For ten fucking months now I've been listening to this!

As annoying and irritating as it is, the constant bitching I can deal with. Don't get me wrong, it drives me up the wall, but I can tolerate it. It's not like I have anywhere to go. I can't just turn the radio up and ignore her either. But like I said, I can accept the whining. But the sobbing fits. These hour long stints locked in the bathroom, Mother consumed with her self pity. Those kill me. "Goddamn it, why am I pregnant." Duh! Do you need a biology lesson, Mother? Or perhaps you need to brush up on your anatomy. And then, "Why me, God?" That one always pisses me off. And worst of all, "Why is this happening to me?" That one really hurts. Doesn't she know I'm her child? All she can think about is herself...that miserable bitch!

I think mommy wants me out of here. But I ain't going anywhere.

Wah. Wah. Wah. "My feet hurt." Wah. Wah. Wah. "My ass is fat." Wah. Wah. Wah. "My boobs are huge."

It never fucking ends! She constantly cries. Who's the baby here?

Wah. Wah. Wah. "I'm hungry." Wah. Wah. Wah. "My back hurts." Wah. Wah. Wah. "I have to pee again."

A broken fucking record. She's as predicable as a game of tic tac toe and her bladder's as hyperactive as a special ed kid who spit out his Ritalin when no one was looking.

I think mommy wants me out of here. But I ain't leaving!

Ten months and counting...and I'm here to stay.

TWO

$\approx$

"It can't be!" Sue Ellen squeezed her eyelids shut, then opened them again. There was no way. It wasn't freakin' possible. She blinked, and blinked again. But the damn thing wouldn't change.

"Fucking positive! How can it be fucking positive?"

Last night she'd gone to Rierson's Drug Store and bought three different home tests. First thing this morning, she'd balanced over the bowl, teetering like a drunken hobo on a busted seesaw, straining like hell to make sure she didn't miss the stick with that first morning urine. What a nightmare that'd be; then she'd have to spend another twenty-four hours in god-awful suspense. They all said the same thing: positive. She was pregnant.

"It's just not possible," Sue Ellen kept telling herself, but the dipstick don't lie. She slammed down the lid—a painful mistake as the noise of plastic smacking porcelain felt like a waffle skillet had been slammed shut on her skull—then sat down on the toilet seat and put her head in her hands. She rubbed her throbbing temples, trying her best to ignore the racket coming from the other side of the bathroom door.

"Holy mother of God…I've been knocked up again."

Sue Ellen paused, staring at the moldy off-white tiles of her bathroom floor, trying to find an answer. Could she really be pregnant with another snot-nosed, sass back, drive-me-up-the-wall, rob me of my youth and beauty, pain in the mother lovin' ass, kid?

Hell no.

Another kid! How could this have happened? She'd

been down this road: three kids in four years, with three different fellas. Here she was, four years since Elie-Dre'd been born, looking to start all over again. The swollen hands and feet. The cravings. The weight. The delivery...lord help her the delivery!

Sue Ellen stood up and reached into the shower, turning the hot water knob as far to the left as it would go. She wanted her troubles to fade the same way her reflection did in a coat of steam that quickly covered the mirror. But when she wiped the mirror, the same pissed-off, sad face was still staring back at her.

She slid the shower curtain to the side, about to get into the hot shower, but she just couldn't shut out the outside world any longer.

"Momma! Open up! Open up, Momma!" The voice on the other side of the door was hollering and banging away at the door with an open hand. "Open up! Open up!"

What choice did she have? The boy would keep yelling until his throat went sore. And he'd keep banging until his hands turned blue. It was Elie-Dre, her youngest. "Momma! I really gotta go!"

"Oh, alright. I'm comin'!" she yelled, even though she knew the boy couldn't hear. No sense bothering with a robe or towel, so she just opened the door and then stepped aside.

Like The Little Engine that couldn't wait another second, Elie-Dre barreled in, his zipper already undone. He whipped out his little manhood and a stream of pee sprayed wildly.

"Goddamn it!" she yelled. Then she grabbed the boy by his round head and turned his eyes towards her. "Lift the seat first," she said, slowly enunciating each word.

"Sorry, Momma. I gotta go real bad."

"Well wipe the seat with toilet paper when you're finished." She gestured with her hands to the roll of toilet paper and moved her arms around in a circular motion.

"Yes, Momma."

Sue Ellen stepped into the hot shower and let the scalding water run down her body. She turned around and the heat soothed her aching back.

She saw Elie-Dre's light brown back running off. The kid forgot to flush again. Elie-Dre could really drive her nuts. It wasn't easy to communicate with him, being born with no ears and all, but he was still her baby.

Barely a second or two passed when she heard the pitter-patter of her middle child scurrying into the bathroom. She peered out, around the shower curtain and saw him facing the toilet, but didn't hear any stream hitting the water.

"Elie-Jay, what are you doing?"

"Making pee-pee, Momma," he said in a screechy whisper.

She looked down at the floor and saw a puddle of piss piling up. She smirked and shook her head, then returned to her shower.

Sue Ellen closed her eyes and faced right into the stream of hot water, allowing it to rush down her body. She reached for the soap and began to slowly wipe her midsection. For just a split second, it soothed her.

"Momma! What a mess it is in here!"

It was Kimi-Sue, her eldest child. She too needed to pee and it didn't take long for her to start bitching about the yellow pond on the bathroom floor.

"Wipe the seat, honey."

"Yuk! It's so gross. I ain't touching all that piss."

"Don't talk like that."

"Why not? That's what it is, ain't it? It's piss. That's what Cleve calls it."

"Well just 'cause Cleve talks like that, don't make it okay for you to."

"Momma, I gotta pee. Okay, now help me!"

"Just wipe the seat."

"Momma!"

"Alright! Fine."

Sue Ellen stepped out of the shower—her wet body dripping water on the floor, diluting the yellow with streaks of clear water—and grabbed a handful of toilet paper. She flung it down on the floor and it began to soak up the pee. She took another pull at the toilet paper roll and used the sheet to wipe down the seat.

"There." She shot her mean-look at her daughter; she had to be firm with Kimi-Sue or else she'd complain all day. "Now make your pee-pee and get ready for school."

"Yes, Momma," Kimi-Sue replied; the words were polite but the tone most certainly was not.

"Don't sass me."

Kimi-Sue sat down on the seat and began to pee, looking away from her mother as she did.

Sue Ellen got back into the shower and flipped the curtain closed as she exhaled her frustration in a cloud of steamy air.

The toilet flushed and surprisingly, Kimi-Sue remembered to close the door behind her when she left the room.

"Finally! Some peace and quiet."

The hot water was slowly turning to lukewarm but that didn't make no difference. Sue Ellen was alone. Just herself and her shower. If only it could last forever.

She washed her entire body, slowly, savoring every

second she was alone. When she shut off the water, she expected to hear silence. Instead, she was startled to hear the loud and obnoxious sound of Cleve passing gas on the toilet.

"Cleve! When did you come in here?"

"Honey, when a man's gotta take a dump, he's gotta take a dump."

She shook her head as the stench hit her. "Cleve, that is foul."

He shrugged his shoulders, then looked down at the morning sports pages, which were rumpled between his hairy, muscular legs. Cleve wasn't exactly a looker, but he did have strong legs.

"I need to dry my hair."

"So, who's stopping you?"

"Cleve! It smells in here."

"I'll be done in a minute."

Sue Ellen rolled her eyes and held her nose, then reached over Cleve's lap and picked up her hair dryer. She grabbed her bathrobe and dashed out of the room.

She walked into her bedroom. It was nice to have her own bedroom. Cleve was one pain in the ass, but he provided her with a bedroom. Before she met Cleve, they all slept in one room: all four of them. For a while, they had nowhere to stay at all. But as long as she could put up with his smelly shits and barroom manners, Cleve would always give her a room of her own. It was something.

It was everything.

No more busting her nails at The Route Nine Diner. No more cranky, overtired truckers leaving shitty tips. No more bitchy housewives who complained that the service was too slow or the food was too cold. No more whiny brat kids throwing their half-eaten food on the floor.

No more shaking her ass for smelly old perverts at titty bars. True, she was only twenty-two but after three kids things do start to droop and sag—and anyway, she never was pretty enough to work at one of those high class "Gentleman's Clubs." She had to settle for dumps like The Rump Shaker and Big Bottoms where the guys did whatever the fuck they wanted and the bouncers didn't do shit about it but laugh. No more. No more drunk frat boys she went to high school with coming into the joint and calling her names, snapping her G-string against the crack of her ass, then violently throwing a buck her way as if that somehow made it okay.

No more lap dances and no more twelve-hour shifts. No more coming home reeking of cigar smoke and no more heel spurs from spending too much time on her feet.

No more. No more. No more.

She didn't have to deal with any of it. She had Cleve. And as long as he got his morning blowjob, he was happy.

"Sue Ellen," she heard him call from the bathroom. "Come here, honey."

"Get in the shower, I'll be right there." She put down her hair dryer. No sense doing it now if it was only gonna get wet again.

Cleve whipped out his cock and she took the head into her mouth. The head was always the easy part. On her knees in the shower, she tilted her neck to the side as he cursed and forced his cock in further.

"Goddamn. Work with me, girlfriend."

She wiggled back and forth as he grabbed her by the hair and held her in place just so. She was used to the rough treatment. She got it each and every morning. Cleve said a morning without a blowjob was a wasted morning, and he wasn't happy to waste a morning. So she took care of him first thing, each and every day for the last year and a half now. But this morning she wasn't feeling right. Not right at all. Her stomach wasn't happy.

Sue Ellen pulled away from him and sucked in air.

"Hey!" he said with a smirk. "Don't stop. I ain't done yet."

She forced out a smile and went back to business, despite her stomach churning and burning something awful.

He arched his back and tried to get more than the head into her mouth, which was darn near impossible with the giant kink he had in his dick.

"Fuck!" Cleve was starting to get frustrated again. This happened every morning. "Son of a bitch, I never should have taken that bet."

She couldn't help but gag. She'd already had her morning English muffin and damn if it wasn't about to find its way back up the way it came.

He twisted her neck in a way it just wouldn't go.

"Ouch."

"I'm sorry, baby. But you know how I get."

"It's okay. Does it hurt? It looks really red today."

"One of these days, baby, I am going to get that knot out."

"I know you will."

"I got the last laugh anyway. Those tickets to Smackdown were worth it, I tell ya. And I'll get that knot out if it's the last thing I ever do."

"I know you will."

She did her best to please him. He continued to arch his back and grunt and moan. He muttered swears and when she opened her eyes, his cock looked just awful, a sore shade of

17

red with bulging purple veins.

With one last fierce arch of his back, he shouted, "Fuck!" His entire body convulsed and his manhood quivered. She pulled back and the midsection of his cock, just above the knot was plump like a boa constrictor with a giant rat stuck in its gut. He yanked at it until it popped, and his goo squeezed through the knot and splattered all over like one of those old Bugs Bunny cartoons; you know when Elmer Fudd's shotgun got tied in a knot and black smoke just blew out the sides. One day, she was afraid Cleve's cock might explode the same way.

She looked up at him, and he was tearing and his nose was running. "Thanks, baby," he said.

"Are you okay?"

"Just perfect." He adjusted his junk while she stepped out of the shower. "Where you going?"

She turned on the faucet and splashed her face with water; her open mouth caught some of it and the rest simply hit her face. She was damn sure she was gonna puke. But she didn't.

"Sorry, Cleve. I'm not feeling so good this morning."

"Damn, girl, you know I like it when you finish up the job."

"I'm sorry. Really."

"Fine, whatever."

Trying to ignore the rumble in her belly, Sue Ellen went to her bedroom and dried her hair. When she walked out of her room, she looked out the front window and saw a huge puff of black smoke, and in front of it, a big yellow bus speeding away.

"Kimi-Sue! You missed your bus."

Kimi-Sue came walking out of her bedroom. "Oops,"

she said with a shrug.

"Dammit! I don't have time to drive you to school."

"Why not?"

"Because, I have to drop Elie-Jay off at his school, and Elie-Dre off at nursery school."

"Mommy," Elie-Jay croaked meekly as he walked out of the room he shared with his brother, "today's Tuesday. Elie-Dre don't have school on Tuesdays."

"You're right." She just had too much on her mind. Elie-Dre only went to nursery school on Monday, Wednesday and Friday. "Okay. Let's go. Everyone in the car!"

They walked out and the three kids piled into the Dodge station wagon. She hated the farty-looking thing but it was a real upgrade from the rusty old van they'd called a home for six months before meetin' Cleve.

She couldn't think straight. What the hell was she to do? She had to see the doctor…she had to confirm it. Didn't she?

"Mom! Elie-Dre's pulling my hair!" Kimi-Sue moaned in the background, but Sue Ellen wasn't listening.

Still, as if her mouth was on autopilot, she turned around, looked the boy in the eye and yelled, "Elie-Dre, leave your sister alone!"

"She started it! She took my Sponge Bob."

"Did not!"

"Did too!"

What the hell was she going to do!

"Stop fighting!" the autopilot mouth shouted, even as the brain continued to wander. Keeping one hand on the steering wheel, she leaned over, grabbed the Sponge Bob doll from Kimi-Sue and handed it to Elie-Dre.

How was she going to go to the doctor's office when

she had Elie-Dre all day?   Damn, why couldn't today be a Monday, Wednesday or Friday!   Why did it have to be Tuesday?

"Mommy! Elie-Dre's stretching out my shirt."

Sue Ellen looked into the rearview mirror. Elie-Dre was pulling the strap of Kimi-Sue's halter top and letting it snap.

"Stop it!" Kimi-Sue whined, then slapped his arm.

She turned back around and grabbed the boy's chin. "Elie-Dre! Leave your sister alone."

Elie-Dre quickly turned his head and shoulders away from his sister, towards the driver's side back window. Sandwiched between her brothers, Kimi-Sue looked straight ahead, her face red and lips pursed together. Like one of those Hollywood movie stars, she twisted her head and did a hair flip while biting her bottom lip.

Then, out of the corner of her eye, Sue Ellen caught a glimpse of Elie-Jay sitting quietly, crouched in the corner on the passenger side, barely taking up any space. In fact, he was leaning against the door so as not to disturb his sister. Open in front of him was a Dr. Seuss book, which he was reading quietly. What would she do without her Elie-Jay? He was such a good boy.

"Kimi-Sue, move over a little," Sue Ellen said sternly. "Give your brother some room."

"I don't have any room!"

"I'm fine, Momma. I have plenty of room."

"Shut up, froggy!"

"Kimi-Sue, don't you talk to your brother that way. Now move!"

"Fine!"

"Elie-Jay, don't lean against the door like that. It's

dangerous."

"Okay, Momma."

She whipped up the circular path to Heinz Kindergarten and stopped, right in front of Phyllis, the crossing guard.

"Would ya slow down, please!" Phyllis snapped as she hop-stepped over on her one leg, using her long-pole stop sign as a crutch.

"Sorry, Phyllis."

"You gotta be careful. There's kids around!"

"I know. You're right."

Phyllis stood up straight, leaning against her sign while lighting a cigarette. "Slow down!" she said, cigarette dangling and smoke dragon-fuming out her nostrils.

"Bye, Momma," Elie-Jay said as he opened his door.

"Bye, sweetie. Mommy loves you."

"Love you, too," he said, then shut the door.

She watched him hop, skip and jump up the asphalt path and once he was to the door, she waved to Phyllis and pulled out. Phyllis didn't wave back.

Once back on the road, Sue Ellen gunned it through traffic. She didn't know why. What was the big hurry? She just couldn't think straight. Finally, she reached The Hodges School, Grades 1-6. Next year Elie-Jay would go there, too, thank goodness—one less stop she'd have to make on days like these.

"Okay, Kimi-Sue. Have a nice day."

Kimi-Sue slid across the seat and opened the door. Without saying a word, she stood up, shot an evil eye at her little brother, then slammed the door shut.

Sue Ellen sighed, then drove away, muttering, "She has her father's temper."

ॐ

Not knowing what else to do, Sue Ellen drove straight to Dr. Kurtsworth's office. She slid cockeyed into a parking space, ignoring her squealing tires, and jumped out of the car.

"Come on, Elie-Dre!" she shouted as she opened the door and yanked him out.

They walked up the steps and into the waiting room. Sue Ellen stepped right up to the window that separated the waiting room from the reception area.

Rosalie, the leather-tanned, gum chewing receptionist sat behind a large Formica desk. She didn't look up as she asked, "Can I help you?"

"Hi, Rosalie," Sue Ellen said as she panted, trying to get air back into her lungs.

Rosalie half looked up, still busy with something behind the desk, and between cow-chews and bubble snaps said, "Miz Biddle, you don't have an appointment today."

"I know, Rosalie, but I have an emergency. I need to see Dr. Kurtsworth as soon as possible."

"Well you're not in the book." *Chew. Snap. Chew.*

"I know I'm not in the book, Rosalie. But this is very important. I can wait if I have to, but I really need to see the doctor."

"I win," a squeaky voice said from behind the desk.

"Fine. Best two outta three." Rosalie finally looked Sue Ellen directly in the eyes. *Chew. Snap. Chew. Snap.* Rosalie sighed, then said, "What's the emergency, Miz Biddle? Are you okay?"

"Yes, I'm okay…I mean…I'm not okay. I'm not dying or anything."

"X in the top left corner," she said then turned to Sue

Ellen. "Just tell me the problem, please." *Chew. Chew. Snap. Snap.*

Sue Ellen looked over her shoulder. Elie-Dre was sitting in a chair, his legs dangling about as he hummed the Sponge Bob theme, horribly out of key.

"It's personal," she whispered.

"Okay, Miz Biddle. You'll have to come back this afternoon." *SNAP!*

"This afternoon! I just can't wait."

"I'm afraid you're gonna have to." *Chew. Snap.*

"I said this is an emergency!"

"I win again," the squeaky voice chimed. Sue Ellen stretched out her neck to see a tiny man behind the desk with a small piece of paper and pencil in his hand.

"Fuck me!" Rosalie screamed. "You cheat."

"Do not."

"Cheater! I hate you."

"Poor sport."

Sue Ellen said, "Excuse me, but this is an emergency."

Rosalie turned to Sue Ellen and said, "This is why you never play tic tac toe with a midget. They always cheat!"

"I do not cheat," the little man said. "And I prefer little man."

"Shut up you cheatin' midget."

"Little man! You hear me? Little man. Little man. Little man."

"Well beat it you cheatin' little man. Go clean up the examination rooms."

"Fine!" He ran towards the door and Rosalie flung her gum at him.

"Excuse me Miz Biddle. He is useless." She stuck a fresh piece in her mouth. "We'd fire him but Dr. Kurtsworth

23

is petrified of lawyers. Anyway, you were saying."

"Yes. I said it was an emergency."

"If it's a genuine emergency, then we can call an ambulance." She blew a quick bubble as she looked down at her appointment book. *POP!* "Otherwise, I have an afternoon cancellation at four o'clock. Why don't you come back then."

Sue Ellen breathed heavily as she bit her lip. Then said, "I really need to see Dr. Kurtsworth."

"Miz Biddle, Dr. Kurtsworth is at the hospital delivering a baby right now. He'll be back around three. If you really need to see him, come back at three and I'll try to get you in."

Sue Ellen shook her head, wondering why Rosalie didn't just say that in the first place. "I can't make it at three. I have to pick up my kids from school."

"Then how about four. I have a cancellation at…"

"I know. Okay. I'll be back at four. Thank you."

Out of the corner of her eye, Sue Ellen saw Rosalie nodding while shoving another stick of spearmint gum into her mouth and flicking the green wrapper aside. Sue Ellen grabbed Elie-Dre by the arm and pulled him out the door.

Sue Ellen pulled up to Heinz and Elie-Jay walked over. Before he could get in, Kimi-Sue jumped out.

"Get in the car, Kimi-Sue!" Sue Ellen rolled down her window and shouted. "Let's go!"

"Just a minute, Momma. I see Maribel."

"You can talk to Maribel later. We gotta go!"

Behind Sue Ellen's car sat a line of oversized SUVs and

station wagons, filled with mothers waiting to pick up their children. Some honked their horns.

"I'll be right there!" Kimi-Sue shouted.

"No! Come now!"

The girls continued talking and giggling as if Sue Ellen wasn't there. She turned and looked in the backseat. Elie-Jay began reading Dr. Suess and Elie-Dre was hollering at Sponge Bob. Then she looked at the clock. It read: 3:06.

"Kimi-Sue. It is time to go. Mommy has an appointment!"

Sue Ellen pulled the car over to the side; there was no shoulder so she softly thumped up onto the curb, then put the car in park.

"I'll be right back boys."

Sue Ellen stepped out of the car and the parade of SUV-driving soccer moms began loading and driving off, swerving around her car and shooting dirty glares her way.

"Kimi-Sue! Get back this instant!"

Kimi-Sue and Maribel ran in the road. Phyllis hobbled over and shouted, "Stop!" The parade of SUVs all stopped. Horns honked and arms flailed.

Sue Ellen ran towards them.

"You girls be careful!" Phyllis shouted.

Kimi-Sue grabbed the stop sign.

"Hey! Give that back to me."

"Give that back this instant," Sue Ellen said, still running over to try and catch them. But the kids ran faster.

Kimi-Sue tossed the sign to Maribel. Sue Ellen tripped and scraped her knees on the asphalt.

"Shit!" Her knees began to bleed.

"Give me that back!" Phyllis was huffing for air as she hopped after them.

Phyllis leaped at Maribel, and Maribel tossed the sign to Kimi-Sue. Then Phyllis grunted, and pogo-sticked back the other way.

The horns continued to honk as the game of monkey-in-the-middle continued. The line of SUVs stood still.

Sue Ellen got up and rubbed pebbles from her knees. "Enough! Give the sign back."

"Yes, Momma," Kimi-Sue said. She reached out and handed the sign to Phyllis. As Phyllis went to grab it, Maribel bent over on all fours and stood behind Phyllis. Kimi-Sue gave Phyllis a little push, and she stumbled over Maribel's back, plunging to the ground, cursing.

Sue Ellen grabbed Kimi-Sue and yanked her. "Get in the car. Now!" She bent over and helped Phyllis up. "I'm so sorry."

"Yeah. Yeah. You need to teach those brats manners!"

"I know. I'm really sorry."

Sue Ellen walked towards her car. Martha, the meter maid was standing in front of her car, writing her a ticket. She held the ticket book in her one good arm and wrote with her teeth.

"Goddammit!" She opened the car door and thrust Kimi-Sue inside. "Get in." She turned to Martha, who was ripping off the ticket with her teeth. "I'm sorry. Can you give me a break?"

"Sorry. Once the ticket's been ripped, you gotta pay." Her voice was slightly muffled as she spoke with her mouth full. She put the ticket book in her mouth while pulling the ticket out of her teeth, and used her hand to tuck the ticket under the windshield.

Sue Ellen grabbed the ticket from between her windshield wiper as she looked at her clock.

It read: 3:17. She was going to have to hurry across town through midday traffic.

THREE

YAWWWWWWN.

That was a pretty good nap. What the hell is that noise? Man, let me rub the chunky gunk from my eyes and pick some goop outta my ears.

Would someone tell me what the fuck is going on here? It's the girl. She is making some kind of fuss. What's that? Oh, she doesn't want to come along with Mommy to the doctor's office. Poor, poor wuddle baby. Life is just so hard.

"I don't wanna go!"

Man! What a freakin' drama queen my big sister is... well half sister, or something like that. Anyway, I hear her carrying on and on. I feel the car start moving. Thank god. I hate sitting still. It upsets me, and then I have to kick around and try to find a good position. At least when things are moving I feel comfortable. But this kid won't give it up.

"I don't wanna go! I don't wanna go! I don't wanna go!" *she keeps on yelling. No, not yelling, shrieking like a spoiled little banshee. If she doesn't stop soon, I swear I'm gonna rip right out of Mommy's belly and beat the shit outta her.*

"Mommy, why are we going to the doctor's office?" *It's the little one talking. If you call that talking, what he does: that pitiful lisp that sounds like he's spraying half a gallon of spit with each syllable. And he never talks—he hollers. He must give Mommy huge headaches. Shit, I've only been around six weeks and I'm already sick of his voice. I wish he would just shut up!* "I don't wanna go to the doctor's office

29

either."

"I don't have a babysitter. You guys are just gonna have to deal. For Mommy's sake. Please."

"Okay, Mommy. We'll be good." *It's the middle one. How can she even hear a word he says with that whispery voice and the other ones yelling over him all the time. What a little kiss ass he is. A sissy mary too. I bet the little one could beat his big brother's ass any freakin' day of the week. But whatever.* "Kimi-Sue, Mommy needs to go to the doctor. It's very important."

"But I don't wanna go! I want to play with Maribel! I don't want to sit in the doctor's office. I want to go home and play with Maribel!"

"Kimi-Sue, stop it!" *Mommy snaps and that whiny little bitch of a sister shuts her trap. The little prick quiets down too. Way to go, Mommy! Now maybe I can finish up my nap. I was having a nice dream about pooping and puking, too. I hope they shut up so I can get back to it.*

Yawwwwn. Big stretch.

What is it this time? Can't an embryo get some rest around here! Fuckin' aye!

Okay, well I don't hear those bratty kids, thank freakin' heavens. But something ain't right in my world. What is Mommy up to now?

"Dr. Kurtsworth, I think I'm pregnant."

"Really? Why would you think that?"

"I took a test. Several of them. And they all came out positive. I can't understand it. It just can't be!"

"You took a test."

"Yes. Several."

"Then you're pregnant."

Duh! You sure are a genius, doc. How many years of medical school did it take to figure that one out? I love the way this guy talks. Real slow and deliberate. Each word is labored over as if he's out of breath or just thinking real hard or something.

"Are you sure, Dr. Kurtsworth?"

"Of course."

This doc is a trip. How much does he bill for this? No wonder the healthcare system is broke.

"But how can you be so sure?"

"You will never get a false positive with those tests. Occasionally a false negative, but never a false positive. Trust me."

"Oh, no."

What do you mean, oh, no, Mommy?

"How can that be? I can't be pregnant."

"It's unusual. Let's check you out." *I hear some ruffling.* "Here. Go in the bathroom and try this one."

"Another test? What for?"

"Just to be sure. I'll take some blood as well. Run a few tests."

"Fine."

Easy with the squatting, Mom. This is uncomfortable. What is she trying to piss me out. Don't push so hard!

"Ouch!"

Sorry, Mom, but you started it.

"Goddammit, I can't piss," *she moans. I feel her bouncing around, then hear the door slam.* "Doctor, I just can't seem to go."

"It's okay, Sue Ellen. Just relax."

"I can't."

"Fine. Just go sit down and we'll take some blood."

"Okay."

Ooo, I felt that.

"What am I going to do?"

"What do you mean?"

"I mean, I want to get rid of it."

IT! I ain't no it, Mommy.

"Okay, we can discuss that option."

"No. There is no discussion. I want it taken care of. I can't have another kid."

"Very well, Sue Ellen. Take a few days to think it over, and by then your blood work will come back and we can formulate a plan."

"The plan is formulated, doctor. I want this taken care of."

"Fine. Call me in a few days when the test results come in."

"No! Now. I want this taken care of now!"

MOMMY! Does that mean what I think it means?

"Okay, try these pills. They will cause uterine contractions so you will naturally evacuate the contents. Perhaps you won't need more surgery."

"Okay."

"If they don't work, then we'll explore surgical options."

"Okay."

FOUR

∾

She finally got the two brats and the good boy to bed, and Sue Ellen was ready for sleep herself, but she knew that wasn't gonna happen.

"Oh, man," she groaned as she leaned back in bed while massaging her aching feet. "What a horrible day." Dr. Kurtsworth's pills didn't work. She was sure of it. She couldn't even keep them down, much less let the medicine go to work.

Cleve walked in with just a tattered robe on. The same one he wore every single night. She bought him a new one for his birthday last year but he liked this one: once navy blue but now faded and closer to blackish/purple, ripped along the back so a hint of hairy ass crack showed, the sides had strings hanging down. It smelled funky too.

"When are you going to wear that nice robe I bought you?"

"I like this 'un."

"But the other one is nice."

"But it ain't this 'un. This 'un's comfy," he said as he reached in the back hole and scratched his butt.

Sue Ellen shook her head as she sat up in bed. He leaned over towards her with a crooked grin and put one knee up on the bed. He tried to kiss her but she turned her head to the side.

"Come on, Sue Ellen, you know I hate to waste a good evening."

A blowjob in the morning and sex at night. It was just part of the deal with Cleve.

"Okay, let me take a bath first."

"Well, get to it then," he said, smacking her ass playfully as she got up to walk away.

Sue Ellen ran the bath hot, almost scalding and yet soothing as she sat down in it. She leaned back letting her legs rise out of the water in order to get as much of her midsection underwater as possible. Damn, her tummy hurt.

The last thing she wanted to do was have sex with Cleve. She was sore all over, stressed out as hell and her stomach was queasy again. But when she sat back in the bath and thought it through, the truth was, there was one thing she wanted to do even less than have Cleve's two hundred and fifty pound hairy frame bounce on top of her for two and a half minute: and that was tell Cleve she was pregnant.

Cleve was lying in bed when Sue Ellen walked back into the bedroom. His smelly robe was in a ruffle in the middle of the floor. She hung her own robe up on a hook attached to the door, then stepped over his robe and climbed into bed. She turned off the light, then lay back.

He went to work and she turned her autopilot on and mechanically shifted and twisted along with him. He was a little rough, but nothing out of the ordinary. As he grunted, trying mightily to squeeze his cock inside her past the knot, her mind went elsewhere.

Oftentimes, while having sex with Cleve she couldn't help but think about her father. They had a lot in common—Cleve and Daddy. They were a lot different in ways too, but she couldn't help but notice the obvious similarities: like their age. Cleve was fully double her age, just having celebrated his forty-third birthday a few weeks back. But the more she thought about it, they were nothing alike. Cleve was more like her first boyfriend, Justin Lawrence.

Sue Ellen got to thinking about her fourteenth birthday, walking down the hall of Bartlett Junior/Senior High School, her hands cluttered with books. A loud gang of boys, each wearing blue and white football jackets, walked towards her.

"Hey, Sue Ellen!" they said as they rushed past, their voices all a blur in unison.

At the back of the pack, he stood. Justin Lawrence. Blond curly hair beautifully gelled. Chiseled cheeks and pearly-white smile.

"Hey there, baby girl," he said as he smirked and tilted his head sideward.

"Hi, pumkin pie," she said softly.

"Pumpkin pie!" one of the boys yelled mockingly.

Sue Ellen blushed.

Justin didn't. He yelled, "Shut up, punk!" Then he scowled at Sue Ellen and said, "I told yew not to call me that."

"Sorry, sweetie."

"And don't be callin' me that neither."

"Okay."

"Not sweetie. Not honey pie. And definitely NOT pumpkin pie! Got it?"

"Yes."

"Now you know what I like to be called, don't ya?"

"Yeah."

"Then call me it from now on." His tone turned soft, as he smiled and said, "I'll see you later, baby girl. And we'll celebrate your birthday right proper."

"Okay."

"Okay, what?"

"Okay, Big Bad Baby Daddy."

"That's more like it. Bye now."

He hustled off after his pals.

Later that night, standing in front of her full-length mirror that stood tall in her bedroom, she clumsily applied mascara and waited for Justin. Soon, Sue Ellen heard the roar of exhaust and knew Justin's old pickup, holey muffler and all, was quickly approaching. She walked downstairs as she heard the doorbell ring.

"Hiya, Baby girl," Justin spoke through her mother as if she hadn't opened the door for him.

Sue Ellen walked towards him and said, "Hi..." she paused and glanced at her daddy with the corner of her eye; he sat in his favorite chair in front of a loud football game, just barely louder than Justin's idling truck outside, "...Big Bad Baby Daddy."

Justin smiled, "That's my girl."

She walked towards him and said, "Bye, Daddy."

He scratched his faded ship's anchor tattoo on his shoulder, exposed through his stained white tank top and said, "You kids have a nice time now."

As they walked out to the truck, Justin said, "Yer daddy sure is a strappin' strong fella, ain't he."

Sue Ellen's eyes lit up and she said, "He's the best."

Justin hopped up into the cab of his once blue but now rotted rust-colored Ford. Sue Ellen stepped up gingerly in her pretty, high-heeled shoes and climbed in.

They didn't say much on the ride, as they couldn't hear each other over the noise. When they pulled up in front of Justin's trailer, Sue Ellen said, "I thought we wuz going out fer dinner."

"Nah. I got alls we need here. Got some good scotch and nice music."

"But I'm hungry."

"Sue Ellen, you don't need no goddamn food you fat bitch!"

"Do you think I'm fat," she pouted while fidgeting in her size two dress.

"Nah. Of course not." He opened his door, slammed it and shouted, "Come on!"

Justin walked up the three-step stoop into his trailer. She followed close behind. It was dark, but Justin didn't turn on any lights.

"You sit down," he said as he walked into the next room.

As her eyes adjusted to the darkness, she made out the outlines of the couch. She felt her way along and there was shit all over it: newspapers, boxes and who-the-hell knew what else. She pushed it aside and sat.

"Goddamn it, Momma!" she heard him yell from the next room. He walked back and said, "Momma drank all the scotch, but I've got some Wild Irish Rose somewhere 'round here. Lemme get it."

"Where is she?"

"Who? Momma? Don't worry 'bout her. She's passed out in the other room. She took a bottle of them Viconexes and washed 'em down with my last bottle of nice scotch. She won't be botherin' us none."

"Where's yer daddy?"

As he shuffled through the shelves, he said, "Aw, he ain't been home fer weeks. I think he's gone westbound to Texarkana to pick up a truckload'a Coors." Sue Ellen heard more shuffling, then he shouted, "Euree-eka! Found it."

He clicked on a lamp next to the couch, then sat down next to her. Justin cracked open the bottle of white wine and took a slug. "Ahhh. I prefer it cold but I gotta hide shit or Momma'll drink it on me. Here."

Sue Ellen took the bottle from Justin and sniffed it.

"Drink it." He paused. "It's good."

She took a tiny sip. It was bitter...or sweet....or something. It basically just tasted like warm piss.

"Come on. Have a real sip." As Sue Ellen took another small sip, he grabbed the bottom end of the bottle and forced it upwards so the wine ran into her throat, and down the sides of her face. "That's it! Drink it, dammit! Guzzle that shit down."

She gulped as best she could but felt a tickle at the bottom of her throat, and gagged, then spit up a mouthful of wine.

"Goddammit, Sue Ellen. Yer wasting it. That's the last bottle in the house."

"I'm sorry, Big Bad Baby Daddy."

He held the bottle up to the light; there was about a third of the bottle left. "GODDAMNSONOFABITCHIN-MOTHERFUCKINSHITASS! How am I gonna get a buzz on this?"

"I'm really sorry, sweetie pie."

"What?"

"I...I mean, I'm sorry Big Bad Baby Daddy."

He shook his head while biting the side of his cheek, then leaned his head back and sucked down the last of the Wild Irish Rose. Once done, he tossed the bottle aside and it clanked around the floor, but didn't break.

Justin walked into the next room and Sue Ellen heard banging and rattling. He came out, arms full of football equipment, and dropped it in a heap at her feet.

"Put that on. 'kay. I'll be right back."

He started to walk away when she asked, "What ya mean?"

"Put it on, stupid! Just put on my football outfit. You do know how to put on a pair of shoulder pads, don't cha?"

She shrugged. "I guess so."

"Good. Now get to it, baby girl."

She bent over and looked at the pile of stuff. What went where? She took off her shoes, then reached back to unzip her dress but had a hard time reaching. Finally, she did and she slid it off. Sue Ellen picked up the padded pants and stepped into them one leg at a time, then tied the shoelace-strap tight. She picked up the shoulder pads and with a little effort, figured out how to fasten them in place. She picked up Justin's white and blue, number 17 football jersey, and struggled to get it up and over the shoulder pads. She couldn't do it. She managed to get the left arm through but the right side hung half on, half off the pad and her arm didn't go through the sleeve of the jersey, instead it hung limply to her side. Lastly, she bent over and picked up his helmet. It was too big for her small head, but she pulled it on anyway, then sat down on the couch.

"Sue Ellen," she heard him call in a high-pitched, sing-song voice, "here I come!"

Justin pranced in on his tippy toes. He was wearing a pink, frilly tutu, like she wore as a kid the one summer she took ballet class. As he danced closer, she could see white gunk all over his face.

"What's on yer face, Big Bad Baby Daddy?" she asked.

"What? That's kazibuki makeup, like the orientiles wear. Don't you know nuthin', baby girl?"

"What's an orientile?"

"Shit, you really dumb, Sue Ellen. Ain't you ever seen

one?"

"I don't think so. Maybe on TV. I've never been outta Hokeyville."

"Hey! You ain't wearin' the jock strap. You can't be no football player with no jock strap." He bent over and picked up a funny looking belt and handed it to her. "Put it on."

She took it from him and looked at it. Then she looked up, unsure of what to do.

"Step into it. It's a fuckin' jock strap, dammit."

She shook her head, and he grabbed it from her hands.

He pulled it wide and said, "Just step into it. You can wear it over your pants."

She stepped into the belt one leg at a time, then he yanked it up high.

"That's better. Now you be the center, and I'll be the quarterback. Got it?"

She shrugged.

"Shit. I ain't never seen a girl as dumb as you, Sue Ellen." He placed a football on the floor in front of her and said, "Bend over and touch the ball. Okay?"

She bent over and grabbed the ball.

"No, like this." He twisted her at the waist and leaned her forward. "That's it. Just stay like that."

"It's a little uncomfortable, Big Bad Baby Daddy."

"Just stand still, baby girl." He walked over to the corner of the room and turned on some music. It piped through the house and looking backward between her legs, she watched him get on his tippy toes and twist, then turn, and jump, then turn fully around. "Ain't this good, Sue Ellen? I'm a good dancer, ain't I?"

"You sure are, Big Bad Baby Daddy."

"I can fly!" he said as he hopped and leaped through the

air. "Now when I say hike, you snap the football. Got it?"

"I think so."

"Good." The music was building and getting louder and Justin's leaps and jumps got higher along with the rising volume and tempo of the tune. "Blue twenty-two!" he shouted as he spun. "Blue twenty-two. Omaha. Omaha. Red one-fifty counter trey." He paused and stood right behind her. He wedged his right hand between her legs, pressing the hard cup of the funny belt against her butt crack. "Hike!"

Sue Ellen pulled the ball up and Justin grabbed it from her, then knocked her face first to the ground and ran around the room. The lamp crashed and books and boxes flew about. Justin ran the length of the doublewide, dodging some obstacles while knocking others over. Finally, a small black stepstool caught his toes and he plunged across the carpet, coming to rest in front of her.

Through heavy breath he shouted, "First down!"

Unsure of what to do, Sue Ellen paused and listened to him huff and puff. Then, she started clapping and cheered, "Yay! Way to go team!"

"What are you, stupid? You're the center, not the cheerleader. Come on. Let's run another play."

"Okay."

"But this play might get rough. Put your jockstrap on right."

She shrugged. "Okay." She slid the funny belt off, and then the pants.

"The jockstrap should be under the underwear."

"Okay." She slid off her panties, then she stepped into the funny belt and leaned over for her panties.

"You won't be needing them."

"Okay."

Justin handed her the ball then said, "Let's go. Run it again." He walked back to the stereo and re-cued the music to the beginning of the same song as she bent over and gripped the football.

Justin twinkle-toed around to the music and as the song built up, he leaped and jumped and turned along with it. The song again grew louder and played faster. He stood behind her and yanked the bottom of his tutu to the side. In the dark, she could see the outlines of his cock. She'd never seen one up close before, but even looking backwards and upside down, it looked pretty big.

"Blue twenty-two. Blue twenty-two." He grabbed his cock with one hand and leaned in close to her; his other hand wedged between her legs, the top end of his palm pressing into her bare butt. "Omaha. Omaha. Red one-fifty. Hike!"

Sue Ellen pulled the football up towards him, which he grabbed and quickly flipped aside. He rammed his cock into her virgin insides, and she stumbled from his weight. He leaned into her and she steadied herself as best she could. He grabbed the side of her shoulder pad with one hand and yanked the back of the funny belt with the other then bounced her into him. Her arm gave way from his weight and they both fell forward. The facemask of the helmet hit the ground and her head tilted as she re-steadied herself with her arms.

Justin began singing loudly along with the music in some weird language she couldn't understand. Then fiercely, and loudly he yelled, "Eureeeeeee-eeeekkka!"

Cleve moaned, his usual agonizing moan. Sue Ellen felt him quiver and heard him whispering curses. He rolled over, sweating, while trying to squeeze the clog out of his hose.

Nine months after she and Justin'd tore up the doublewide, little Kimi-Sue was born. And here it was, just seven years and three kids later, and she had another kid growing in her belly.

"GODDAMNSONOFABITCHINMOTHERFUCKIN-SHITASS!" Sue Ellen said to herself. It was a whisper, but a firm whisper.

"What, honey?" Cleve asked, finally starting to smile as his cum slid slowly out his pee hole.

"Nothing, Cleve. Just go to sleep."

And he did. Sue Ellen, however, didn't. She lay awake for hours, wondering how in the hell she could be knocked up again.

FIVE

Yawwwwn.

What now, Mommy? Where are we going? Man am I hungry. When was the last time Mommy ate anything? Is she trying to starve me? She tried to kill me with that poison but I made her puke the pills up. Does she think I'm stupid?

Hey, I recognize that patronizing, deliberate voice. Are we back at that doctor's office?

"Okay, Sue Ellen have you followed the pre-op instructions?"

"Yes, Dr. Kurtsworth."

"Okay, then. Up into the stirrups, and I'll go get the nurse."

What are they up to? I don't like the sound of this.

"Now don't worry a bit, Sue Ellen. This won't be much different than a regular exam. I'm going to start by inserting the speculum into your vagina. Just like for a pap"

"Okay."

Damn. Feels a bit drafty in here all of a sudden. Someone shut the door, please.

"Clean the area please, Nurse."

"Yes, Doctor."

"Now, I'm going to give you a local anesthetic. No big deal at all, Sue Ellen."

"Okay, doctor."

Hmmm. That feels kinda good. I could go for a nice nap, suddenly.

"Sue Ellen, we are going to use the manual vacuum.

That should be the simplest method."

"Okay, Dr. Kurtsworth. Whatever you think is best. I just want this over with."

"I'm going to insert a small syringe into your uterus. It will be done in a few minutes."

What the...man...who pulled out the drain plug? The tide is flowing down all of a sudden. What's with the slurping noises?

"I think I've got it, Sue Ellen."

Back off, Jack! Shit man! Lay off my fluid. Stop pokin' my head with that you bastard!

Poke! Poke! Poke! That freakin' doctor is poking my head and then sucking in. What is he trying to do to me? I've got a thick skull and all, but that thing he's using has some pull to it.

Knock it off!

"Ouch!"

"What's the matter, doctor?" *I hear the nurse ask.*

"Nothing, just got a funny vibration. That's all. Never felt anything quite like that. Nurse, get the machine."

That's better. Get that needle up outta here!

"What's wrong, Doctor?"

"Nothing at all, Sue Ellen. Nurse, let's get an ultrasound on this."

What is that putz up to?

"Nurse, I don't believe it."

"What is it?" *I hear the nurse and Mommy say together.*

"The fetus has already developed a head."

"Huh, that's weird," *the nurse says.*

"Dr. Kurtsworth, what's going on?" *Mommy whines.*

"It's okay, Sue Ellen. But we are going to need the

vacuum machine. It's very routine. The pregnancy is too far along for the manual vacuum, that's all."

"Okay. Just end this."

Now what? That is way too big to be a needle. What the fuck is that tube?

"Don't worry, Sue Ellen. The vacuum is actually very gentle."

"Okay, Dr. Kurtsworth."

Holy shit! What is that noise? Turn off that fucking jackhammer, doc! You're freakin' killing me. My ears are barely even formed yet. Are you trying to make me deaf for life? SHUT THAT NOISE OFF, MAN!

Goddamn. What's with the Hoover. My four strands of stubbly hair barely busting out of their follicles are getting yanked towards the opening. Would you leave me alone? Damn! These hurricane winds are too much. I'm grabbing hold of Mommy's slippery sides but it ain't easy to get a firm grip on this greasy thing. Especially with all of Mommy's inner goop whizzing by my head.

This is messed up, Mommy. Messed up. Give a brother a chance to grow some arms and legs.

"Nurse, we are going to have to do a D&C."

"What's going on, Dr. Kurtsworth?"

"Just relax, Sue Ellen. Normal complications."

"Complications?"

"The vacuum just isn't removing all the tissue. In order to ensure the pregnancy is fully terminated, I am going to do what is called a Dilation and Curettage. It's very routine. I've done thousands of these."

"Okay."

"But we can't do it today."

"What!"

"For a D&C we use a general anesthesia. For that you need an anesthesiologist. And it's best done at the hospital."

"But I want this over now! I want this thing out of me!"

Well fuck you too, Mommy.

"I know, Sue Ellen. This is traumatic for you. I am going to give you some pills for your pain."

And what about my pain, doc! You think ramming a needle in my head feels good?

Time to get in shape. Fitness. Nothing but wholesome foods in this body. Lots of veggies. Watch the carbs and dairy. If Mommy eats anything else, I am makin' her puke it up. This is war. I am not safe. It's all about survival brother. It's all about beatin' the man before the man beats you. Thousands of different ways they try to kill you every day. Dope, booze and cigarettes. Cars and motorcycles so fast it's a wonder more folks don't die on 'em. Radiation, pollution. Shit, I can go on and on all day. But none of those problems bug me a bit. You, my friend, you could walk out of your house this morning and a metal sign left balancing precariously against a concrete block could just fall right on your head and kill ya, just 'cause some pimple-faced kid didn't do his job correctly. But me, I got a whole different problem. And my problem ain't random like a metal sign, and it sure ain't self induced like suckin' down cigarettes 'til ya can't breath no more.

No sir. That ain't what my problem is.

My mommy is trying to kill me.

GODDAMNSONOFABITCHINMOTHERFUCKINSH-ITASS! My own Mommy wants me dead. That could really weigh on a brother's conscience if you let it. Lay a headtrip on your mind like mad.

But not me. For me, this is motivation. Five hundred sit ups and three hundred push ups, every morning from now on.

If that sonofabitchin' doctor comes after me again, I'll be ready.

WHEN that sonofabitchin' doctor comes after me again...

I will be ready.

No more Mr. Niceguy. No sir. No sir. No siree. I am no longer just a mild mannered developing human form. I am not just tissue and soft pink goopy soon-to-be flesh.

Heck no.

I

AM

SUPERFETUS!

SIX

ॐ

Sue Ellen walked to the door after her late afternoon appointment with Dr. Kurtsworth. Her stomach turned simultaneously along with the doorknob, as she knew she'd find total chaos on the other side of the door.

"Mommy! Mommy!" Elie-Dre yelled as he ran towards her and leaped into her arms.

"Ouch. Easy, honey. Mommy isn't feeling too good."

"Mommy, can I go play at Maribel's house?" Kimi-Sue shouted, trying to be heard over her brother.

"Kimi-Sue, it's almost dinnertime."

"So?"

"So, it's too late to go over to Maribel's house."

"But I wanna go play with Maribel! I wanna play with Maribel, now!"

"Tomorrow."

"No, not tomorrow. Today…Today! Today! Today!"

"Mommy said tomorrow."

"No! Today…Today! Today! Today!"

"Oh, Kimi-Sue. Just stop it." Sue Ellen walked past Kimi-Sue. Elie-Dre followed her still hollering. His shouts and screams were splitting right through her skull.

"Mommy, mommy. Guess what I did today?"

"What?" she said with a loud sigh, still walking away from him as she did. He tailed tightly behind, repeating himself over and over again until she stopped and made eye contact.

"I watched Sponge Bob."

"That's nice."

"I watched Sponge Bob."

"That's nice, honey."

"I watched Sponge Bob Square Pants."

"That's very nice, honey. I'm glad you enjoyed Sponge Bob."

"Mommy! I watched Sponge Bob Square Pants!"

Elie-Dre just kept shouting. Nothing would stop him. Kimi-Sue joined in.

"Mommy, I wanna go to Maribel's house."

"Tomorrow, Kimi-Sue."

"No! Today! I wanna go to Maribel's house today!"

"Mommy! I watched Sponge Bob Square Pants!" he said as he yanked at her pant leg.

"Sue Ellen, what are we having fer dinner?" Cleve asked.

She was about to answer, but couldn't find the energy to talk over the racket.

"Mommy! I watched Sponge Bob Square Pants!"

"I wanna go to Maribel's house today!"

"I watched Sponge Bob Square Pants!"

"I wanna go to Maribel's house today!"

"I watched Sponge Bob Square Pants!"

"Sue Ellen," he said, now whining and raising his voice to try and compete with the kids, "What's fer dinner?"

"I watched Sponge Bob Square Pants!"

"Mommy, I want to go to Maribel's today."

"I watched Sponge Bob Square Pants!"

The boy kept yanking at her pant leg as the girl kept yelling in her ear. The man kept increasing the level of his voice too, not quite yelling, but making sure he was heard.

"Sue Ellen…what are we having fer dinner?"

Out of the corner of her eye, she spotted her sweet and

precious Elie-Jay. Quiet as could be, sitting on his little blue chair with a Dr. Suess book opened in front of him.

So what if a mother wasn't supposed to play favorites. Whoever said that didn't have a son like Elie-Jay. Of course Elie-Jay was her favorite. He was a perfect boy.

Of course Elie-Jay was her favorite. He was her only child born out of love.

Love like she'd only found once in her lifetime. She remembered the day so vividly: Little Kimi-Sue screamed as Daddy asked, "Where's Justin? I'm too old to be babysitting all the time."

"I know, Daddy. Just put her in the swing. He's on his way over."

The door opened, and Justin waltzed in, in full baseball uniform, carrying his mitt, his dirty spikes tracking mud along the linoleum floor.

"Hi, Big Bad Baby Daddy," Sue Ellen said with a smile. She walked towards him.

"Come on, Sue Ellen. You know that name is so last week. Call me the new name."

"I'm sorry. Hi, Big Booby Bobby."

"Yeah, that's better. Come on. Let's go."

Kimi-Sue finally quieted down in her swing. Daddy looked over. "Are you going out, Sue Ellen? I thought Justin was going to watch the baby tonight."

"Now I'm sorry, Mr. Biddle. But I got plans."

"Plans?"

"Scored me two tickets to the smash 'em up derby. Good seats, too."

"You know what," Sue Ellen said. "You can take my seat, Daddy. And I'll stay home."

"I don't think so, Sue Ellen," Justin said. "Maybe we'll

all just stay home. One big happy family."

"Okay."

"Is there a game on tonight, Mr. Biddle?"

"I think so."

"Good. You sit on down there in your favorite chair, and I'll be right back. Gotta get something from my truck."

"You sit down, Daddy. You relax," Sue Ellen said.

Big Mack Biddle walked to his recliner, gave a funny eye to Sue Ellen, peered out his window at Justin, then turned to the TV set.

Sue Ellen thought how handsome her daddy looked in his favorite recliner.

Justin walked back inside, his brown eyes wide and a crooked smile covered his face. He walked up behind Mack Biddle and grabbed his arms.

"Ouch. What are you doing?"

Justin took an elastic doohickey and snapped it to Mack's right arm, then yanked it behind the chair and clasped it tightly to his other hand.

"What in tarnation are you up to, Justin!"

"Sue Ellen, tie up his legs."

Kimi-Sue began to cry again in her swing.

"Why?" Sue Ellen asked. "Why you gotta hurt him?"

"I ain't hurtin' him."

Justin leaned down and took another doohickey clasp and fastened Big Mack Biddle's left leg to the leg of the chair. Then did the same to his right.

Sue Ellen walked over slowly and tilted her head. "Are you okay, Daddy?"

"No. I'm not okay. Get me outta here."

"I'm tired of those googoo eyes you always givin' him," Justin said. "I'm sick and tired of you lovin' him more than me."

"But he's my daddy. You know I love him."

"What in heavens are you talking 'bout?" Big Mack Biddle said.

"Let's go, Sue Ellen. What chu waiting fer?"

Sue Ellen just stood there. Looking at Justin, then at her daddy, then at little Kimi-Sue, then back at Justin.

Justin threw up his arms and cried, "Come on now. I gotta do everything?" He unbuckled Big Mack's belt and pulled at his pants. He looked at Sue Ellen, folded his arms and said, "Well go on. Get to it."

Sue Ellen hiked up her denim skirt, and dropped her panties.

"What the..."

She hopped onto the chair and straddled Big Mack Biddle.

"That's my baby girl," Justin said. "Do it just like we planned. Just like I always promised you. I know'd you wuz hot for your daddy from the first day I met you."

Sue Ellen reached down and grabbed Mack Biddle's big mac; it was twice the size of Justin's, just like the rest of him. She slid it in and began to bounce.

"Sue Ellen," he shouted. "Stop. This is fuckin' sick!"

"Don't listen to him, baby girl. You know it feels right." Justin sat down on the nearby couch and reached into his own pants. Sue Ellen suddenly realized Justin's cock was tiny compared to her daddy's beautifully big bulge.

Sue Ellen looked at her daddy and caressed his face. "Don't you know how much I love you, Daddy?"

"I love you too, baby. But not like this."

His cock slipped out. And Sue Ellen stopped bouncing.

"What?" Justin asked as he cut off the cobra clutch

caressing his cock. "Why you stoppin'?" When she stood up, he answered his own question. "Aw, shit. He done gone limp."

Kimi-Sue wailed in her swing as Big Mack Biddle said, "That's enough, Sue Ellen." He shifted and shook in his bonds, but they were snug and tight. He tried to hop up in his chair, but couldn't quite get to his feet.

"Lick his balls," Justin said.

"Please, Sue Ellen. Don't," Big Mack Biddle said. As she bent down towards him he tried to stand up, and twisted in his chair, but instead fell backwards, taking Sue Ellen to the ground with him.

Justin sat back down on the couch, laughing and began to manhandle his mangy, meager meat again. "Nice one, Big Mack. Now lick his balls and get him hard again, baby girl."

"Yes, Big Booby Bobby."

Sue Ellen licked Big Mack Biddle's bursting balls by the bottom with a blustery boost of bombast.

His voice whined, "Please stop, Sue Ellen, baby, please." But his cock told Sue Ellen a whole other story. It was back at full attention. And Big Mack Biddle's manhood at full attention was just the most awe-inspiring, mesmerizing and beautiful thing she'd ever laid her eyes on.

"That's it, baby girl. Jump back on that shit and ride that horse into the sunset," Justin shouted.

Big Mack continued to wiggle within the fallen-down chair, but he couldn't skirt free. Sue Ellen scuffled up on top of him and grabbed his glorious gong-mallet. Now bigger than before, she could barely get it all in, but as gravity forced her down, his cock went up up up, to the depths of her insides.

Suddenly, she couldn't even contain herself. Her mouth started moving, but she was like that green psycho-kid in the Excrocist and the devil was doin' the talkin'.

"Yeah, Daddy!" she yelled. "Fuck me like a porn star!"

"Woohoo!" Justin yelled as he whacked away at his skinny cock, which looked wimpier and wimpier by the second in the presence of such a gorgeous wonder like her father possessed. "Fuck yer daddy, girlfriend! Fuck him 'til you cum!"

"Oh, please, baby stop," Big Mack Biddle begged, but Sue Ellen just knew he didn't mean it. His cock was too big. It felt too damned good! Of course he wanted more.

Little Kimi-Sue started laughing in her swing. Even she knew what a blast they were having!

"Yeah, Daddy. Fuck me like a porn star! Ram that magnificent man-meat up my waiting wooly woman-cave!"

"Fuck that shit, Big Mack," Justin yelled. "Nail that bitch. Nail her good!"

Sue Ellen stroked Big Mack's sweaty forehead and pushed his bangs out of his eyes. A tear welled in his eyes, and that started her a cryin'.

"I love you, Daddy."

"I love you too, Sue Ellen," he whispered.

"Come on, Big Mack. Blast a load right up in there. I can't hold mine back much longer!" Justin shouted. "I'm gonna cum, and cum hard. Make him cum, baby girl."

"Cum in me, Daddy! Right now. Let it go. Give me a blast of Big Mack's special sauce!"

"Come on, Big Mack!" Justin poured on as he pulled on his puny putty. "I can't hold out much longer. I've got to cum!"

"Cum in me, Daddy," Sue Ellen shouted as she bounced

harder and harder, faster and faster.

Tears ran down Big Mack Biddle's cheeks as his face turned redder and redder. Little Kimi-Sue cheered on in her swing.

"Cum in me, now! Now Daddy. Now!"

And Big Mack Biddle blew the biggest blast of beautiful booty-goo that bloomed into the best boy born: her sweet Elie-Jay.

"Mommy! I want to go to Maribel's house. Now!"

"Mommy. Mommy! I watched Sponge Bob Square Pants today."

"Sue Ellen, what are we doin' fer dinner?"

"Order a pizza," she mumbled, her voice barely heard above the three of them hollering. She walked over to Elie-Jay and kissed his forehead.

Elie-Jay looked up from Horton and the Whos and croaked, "I love you, Mommy." The poor boy had been born without a voice box, and some might say that was a curse. But it was a blessing. The soft tenderness in the buzz of his voice was just so precious.

"I love you too, Elie-Jay."

She never told Daddy that she was pregnant. But once things started to show, he figured it out. Soon Cleve would figure out that she was pregnant again, the same way Daddy did back then. She couldn't hide it much longer. She'd have to just tell him.

SEVEN

❧

One. Two. Three. Four.
Two. Two. Three. Four.
Three. Two. Three. Four.
Four. Two. Three. Four.
Come on! Three more sets!
Gotta keep pushing. Super Fetus needs to stay in shape.
No rest for the weary. That means you too, Mommy.

"Sue Ellen, would you sit still!" *I hear the man say.* "I can't sleep with you tossing and turning like that all the time."

"Well, how do you think I feel? This baby is bouncing around like a Puerto Rican jumping bean."

Sorry, Mommy. Nothing personal. Super Fetus gotta stay in shape. It's a matter of survival.

"Okay, honey," *the man says, his tone becoming all sweet and soft.* "About this baby…"

"What about it?"

"Let's have it."

Atta boy, Cleve. Talk some sense into her.

"No."

"Come on, Sue Ellen. I can afford it."

"Money ain't got a damn thing to do with things."

"Well, what is it, then?"

"I can't deal with another child. I have three kids. I am done."

"Sue Ellen, I don't have any kids."

"You have mine."

"Come on. You know I love yer kids, but it's just not the same. Heck, I'm a lot older than you, Sue Ellen. This

61

could be my last chance."

"I'm sorry, Cleve. I'm meeting Dr. Kurtsworth in the morning to take care of this, once and for all."

"Fine!"

No sleep for me. Like a soldier in enemy territory, I gotta keep one eye open at all times. You never know when that doctor and that bitch Mommy might try something. In the morning, huh? Okay, Mommy. Super Fetus will be ready!

One. Two. Three. Four.

Two. Two. Three. Four.

"Ooooo, my tummy," Mommy groans.

Three. Two. Three. Four. Push it! Push it! Gotta be stronger than that putz of a doctor.

"Sue Ellen, I gotta be up for work in three hours. Could ya please stop hoggin' up all the pillows?"

"Here!" *she says as she throws a pillow at him.*

Four. Two. Three. Four. Don't worry, Mommy. Just two more sets.

"Dammit, I wish this baby'd sit still."

One. Two. Three. Four...

"Okay, Sue Ellen, now just relax while Dr. Ng runs an IV."

It's that freakin' doctor talking. My blood is just boiling from the sound of his voice...or is it just from all the nice warm fluid in here? Ah, no matter. Point is he is pissing me off. I know what he is up to.

And this time, I am ready!

"Please, Dr. Kurtsworth, just get this over with. I need

this taken care of so I can put this entire miserable experience behind me."

Damn Mommy, you sure do know how to make a kid feel all warm and tingly inside.

"Don't worry, Sue Ellen. I will have you in and out of here in no time. Just lie back and relax. Nurse, the speculum."

Damn! There's that breeze again.

"Now the tenaculum."

Ouch! Fuckin' ay, Doc. Give me some room in here. Quit crowding me.

"What's that, Doctor?"

"Don't panic, Sue Ellen. It's just to help dilate things. Are you okay?"

"Yes."

"You seem a bit too coherent, Sue Ellen. The anesthesia should have you just on the verge of falling under."

"I'm fine, Dr. Kurtsworth. Just do the job."

"No, I'd better call Dr. Ng back in here to give you a little more."

"No! Just kill the fuckin' thing. Just finish this. Now!"

"Okay. Okay. Please relax, Sue Ellen. I will take good care of you."

"Thank you. I just want this done."

"Okay. Very good. Nurse, the curette, please."

Bring it on, Doc. Go ahead. Just bring it on.

Here it comes. I see that curved, sharp-looking thing coming at me. He's scraping at the edges of Mommy's insides, looking for me. I'll just squeeze here in this corner. I am very flexible. Maybe if I just really squeeze.

Fuck! He's still coming.

"Nurse, help me out here. I don't think I'm getting

anything."

"What's going on, Dr. Kurtsworth?"

"Just hold still, Sue Ellen. Just hold still."

Ouch! Fuck! Off my toes. That hurts.

Okay. A good soldier knows when it's time to retreat. Get back into my corner. Yeah...that's right, Doc. You can't reach me here, buddy boy.

"This isn't working."

"What? What isn't working?"

"Sue Ellen. Just relax. We are going to try something a little more serious."

"What?"

"It's called a D&E. It's essentially the same thing, but I'll have to use forceps to help grab the tissue."

Tissue? Who you callin' tissue, Doc? I am five pounds, two ounces of fury, and you ain't never gonna get the best of me. This is my home. Stay the fuck out!

"Just do it! I want this done!"

"I know, Sue Ellen. We will take care of you. Nurse, get an ultrasound technician in here."

"Yes, Doctor."

This motherfuckinsonofabitchinSOfuckinB. He is not gonna give up. He is gonna keep coming at me. No more mister nice guy. Come on, Doc. You are gonna be one hurtin' motherfuckin' wannabe baby killer if you try me again.

"Would you look at that baby, Dr. Kurtsworth. Look at the arms and legs...they are so..." *A new voice. Must be that technician.*

"Defined?"

"It's like a fetus on steroids. I've never seen anything like it."

"Me either, but let's get on with it."

Yeah. Come on, biaaaaach!
What the fuck are those. Hey! Get off my leg with those freakin' clippers. Do I look like a rosebush?"
"Okay, let's get the vacuum on."
Shit! What's with the windstorm? Quit yanking at my leg. Goddamn son of a bitchin' bastard.
Gotcha!
"It's broken. The vacuum broke."
Ah ha! It's gonna take more than that to beat me, Doc. But that persistent bastard is still at my leg with those funny looking hooks. Hey! Stop tugging at me.
POP!
FUCK!
"Okay, I've got a piece of something."
Yeah, Doc. My leg you fucker!
"Oh dear, Dr. Kurtsworth. Look at the muscles on that leg."
"Throw it in the bin."
"Yes, doctor."
"What is going on, Dr. Kurtsworth?"
"Relax, Sue Ellen. We are taking care of it."
Man that hurts. Mommy. Mommy, you're supposed to love me and protect me. Not kill me!
I guess she doesn't see it that way, 'cause I hear her yell, "Is it dead yet?"
It? I ain't no it, Mommy!
Now he's yanking at the other leg, but I keep shaking him free. He just keeps after it. I'm grabbing them and yanking the sharp part. Twisting it around Mommy's insides.
"Ahhhhh!" *she's yelling.*
And the doc too. "Ahhhh!"
Get the fuck off of me!

65

"Sue Ellen, are you okay?"

"No! I think you really hurt me."

"Okay. We are going to have to stop. I can't keep doing this. We may really injure you internally."

I hear Mommy start to wail and moan. Hey! Who's the baby here, bitch!

I beat them again! You don't fuck with Super Fetus. Nobody messes with me, man.

Nobody!

EIGHT

~

"Jesus Fucking Christ! Why won't this baby die?" Sue Ellen screamed underneath the cover of the hot shower. She felt horrible about how that sounded, but she yelled it again anyway. "Why won't this baby die?" She looked at her stretched-out stomach and shook her head. It was all she could do. Shake her head back and forth and ask herself, "Why? Why fucking me?"

She felt awful to be talking this way about her unborn child. After all, she had three kids. Even when Kimi-Sue pissed her off something fierce, she couldn't imagine wanting her dead.

But this was different. This baby was not like the others, fuck that maternal instinct bullshit.

"Die! Die! Die!" she shouted while punching her stomach. "Die!" She punched it again and again and again.

As if answering her, her stomach punched back. It was in there punching back at her as if pounding on a wall. *Let me out, Mommy!* she could swear she heard it say. *Stop punching me, you bitch!*

Sue Ellen sat down in the tub and let the water flow from the showerhead onto her face. "I am losing it. I am losing my fucking mind."

"Mommy!" she heard a shout, but this time it wasn't coming from inside her tummy, thank god. "Mommy I have to make pee-pee." It was Elie-Dre.

Did she lock the door? She couldn't remember, but she sure didn't have the strength to get up.

"Mommy! I really gotta go!" Elie-Dre kept on.

"Oh, Elie-Dre," she mumbled. "Elie-Dre. Elie-Dre."

Little Elie-Dre was her baby, and boy could he be a pain in the ass. But it wasn't easy for him.

Sue Ellen thought back to that weird night. She went to Bart's Biker Bar, Bowling Alley and Boot Repair, just a few weeks after Elie-Jay'd been born. She kicked back ripple while Roxie ogled the beer-bellied bikers and buttcrack-showing buffoons in bowling wear.

"Look at him," Roxie said. "I think he is staring at you and he is cute, cute, cute."

Sue Ellen looked over her shoulder to see a big dude with a jiggly gut and Harley Davidson t-shirt. When he saw her looking his way, he raised his eyebrows and puckered his lips.

"That guy?" Sue Ellen asked.

"Yeah," Roxie said while elbowing her. "Why don't you go talk to him."

"I don't think so."

He walked towards them with a very confident walk and a cockeyed look on his face. "Can I get you two darlings a drink?"

"No thanks," Sue Ellen mumbled.

But Roxie spoke over her and said, "You betcha, big man."

"What'll it be?"

"Something strong," Sue Ellen said without looking at him.

"Do you have any friends with you?" Roxie asked.

"Sure, my whole gang's in the back shootin' pool."

"Come on, Sue Ellen. Let's go meet the fellas."

"Nah. I'll stay here."

Roxie looked over with her head turned sideways and a

frown on her face. "Fine," she said, then followed the biker to the back of the bar.

Sue Ellen put back a few more drinks when three odd-looking men came in. Their skin looked burnt; she didn't know what to make of them. Two guys had on shiny shirts and baggy pants. The third guy, walking with a limp, two steps behind the other two, had on a multicolored moo moo like her momma used to wear, a sequined top hat and the biggest pair of sunglasses Sue Ellen had ever seen.

There were two empty stools at the bar next to her, and they walked towards them. The two guys sat down and the third one strutted on up behind. Sue Ellen realized he was wearing a boot on one foot, and on his other was just a holey white sock. He was cute.

The cute one slapped his other boot on the bar and shouted, "What's a nigga gotta do to get a boot fix 'round here?"

Skip, the bartender walked over with squinty eyes and said, "You fellas from around here?"

The three guys looked at each other. The cute one was biting his lip in a seductive way.

"Don't worry, Skip," Sue Ellen said. "They're with me."

"You know these guys, Sue Ellen?"

"Yep, they're my friends. Get them a round on me, Skip. Please."

"Okaaaay," Skip said while throwing up his hands. "You know I'll do anything for you, sweetie."

"Thanks," the cute one said while flicking at the backs of his sunglasses underneath his ears, making them pop up and down. He smiled and his teeth sparkled like shooting stars.

"What are we doing in this here cracker bar, anyway," one of his friends said. The guy had a lot of cheesy gold and silver jewelry and a yellow-toothed smile.

The cute one said, "Can't you see I need my boot fixed." Then he called out, "Yo, Skippy? Where's the shoe man?"

Skip brought over the drinks and said, "He's off tonight." Then he turned to Sue Ellen and said, "You best take your friends elsewhere. The boys in the back are lookin' funny. And they've been drinking since they got here at five o'clock."

"Are you kicking my friends out, Skip?"

"Of course not, Sue Ellen. Just a friendly warning is all. I don't need no trouble tonight."

"Don't worry about me, Skip. I'll be just fine."

The third guy, a short and stocky kid turned to Sue Ellen and said, "Girlfriend, you must be a frosted lucky charm."

"What?"

"A frosted lucky charm, because you look magically delicious!"

She nodded. "Thanks."

The cute one said, "Don't pay him any mind. He needs to learn some manners."

"Hey, Andre. You dissin' me for this white bitch?"

"Come on, knock it off."

"Fuck you, man. Bros before hos. Shit. We out."

The two guys walked out, leaving Sue Ellen alone with Andre. She liked what she saw. His sleeveless moo moo exposed big, solid forearms. His hands were big too.

"So, can a nigga get table dance?" he asked.

"Huh?"

He laughed.

"What are you laughing at?" she asked.

71

"Nothing. Nothing," he said but kept on laughing.

"Stop it," she said as she playfully punched his shoulder. "Stop!"

"No. No. I wasn't laughing at you. I was laughing at me. What I meant was, you pretty."

Sue Ellen smiled, then said, "Like a frosted lucky charm?"

"Nah, nah. Ignore that dumbass. They're my boys and all, but they just can't get out of the hood, you know?"

"The hood?"

"You know, the neighborhood."

"Where's that?"

"Huh?"

She leaned over and sniffed his arm.

"What you doin'?"

"I was just wondering, do you mind?"

"Huh?"

Sue Ellen leaned over again, this time licking his exposed arm.

"What the…"

"I just wondered if you tasted like chocolate."

"Girlfriend, ain't you ever seen a brother before?"

"Brother? I don't have any."

"A black man? Ain't you ever seen a black man?"

"I don't know. Maybe on TV. I ain't never been out of Hokeyville."

"Girl, you sure are strange. But you pretty too. Let's have another round."

"Okay."

Out of the corner of her eye, Sue Ellen saw the bikers staring at them and Roxie egging them on.

"Are you trying to pick me up?"

He shrugged.

"Sue Ellen," Roxie called. "Sue Ellen, come over here, please."

"Do you want to get out of here?" she asked Andre.

"He looked very discreetly over his shoulder and said, "Maybe that'd be a good idea."

"Great, let's go." She waved to Roxie as she walked quickly towards the door. "See you tomorrow, Rox."

"Sue Ellen!" she called, but they were already out the door.

જી

"Sue Ellen," Andre said with the softness of an overnight disc jockey. "That is just the prettiest name I ever heard."

"Aw, shucks. Thanks."

"You are so beautiful."

She walked while he limped down the street. He stopped in front of a minivan. He looked both ways, then slid open the door.

"This yours?" she asked.

"Yeah. I borrowed it."

She stepped in and saw two child car seats.

"Ignore those. Those belong to my nephews."

"Okay."

"You sit in the back there. It's more comfortable."

"Okay."

She climbed over the seats, ducking her head so as not to hit the roof, and plunked herself down on a long seat in the back. He followed.

"Yo, check this out." He grabbed a remote control that was stuck in the wall and pressed a button. A screen lowered in front of them. "D-V-Fuckin' D. Can't beat that shit with a billy-club, yo."

"Cool."

The screen came on and a big red puppet was chirping in a high voice. Andre quickly fumbled with the remote and said, "My fuckin' nephews and this shit." He hit a few buttons and the screen changed. A tiny, bleach-blond girl was inhaling the cock of a large man with chocolate skin. "There. That's what I like." He turned to her. "You like that?"

"Sure. Does it taste like chocolate?"

"Ooo baby, you wanna find out."

"'kay."

He stood up and slid off his underwear, then lay back on the seat. She grabbed his cock. It was pretty big but wasn't beautiful like Daddy's. And it didn't taste anything like chocolate.

"This doesn't taste like chocolate."

"Shee-it. Let's just fuck then."

"Okay."

Sue Ellen tumbled on top of him and took a hold of his tall and tender timber. She lay lovingly on his lumber and lashed out loud.

"Woo wee. This is better than the circus!" she cried.

He looked up at her, his gigantic sunglasses and sequined top hat still in place. "You betcha, girlfriend. You ain't never had nothing like me."

"Never! Never!"

"Ride the painted pony. Ride it good."

"Woo wee! This is better than a day off on a Tuesday!"

"Better than a fresh fade and side of con carne!"

"Better than a fifty dollar tip from a farty old foreman."

"Better than a tax return!"

"Tax return?" she asked.

"Come on. Just fuck me, girlfriend."

"Woo hoo!" Sue Ellen shouted.

Sue Ellen heard shuffling sounds underneath the seats. "What's that noise?"

"Oh, that's nothing."

She leaned over. In the back of the van, his two buddies were huddled in each corner.

"Don't mind them," Andre said.

"I don't."

"You don't?"

"Nah."

"Cool. Come on out, fellas."

They climbed over the seat and plunged down in a heap in the middle of the van. They were wearing bright, sequined gowns that matched Andre's top hat.

"Oh, cool," Andre said. "You boys changed."

"Those are nice dresses," Sue Ellen said.

"You like? Awesome. Get out the wigs boys."

Andre jumped up and tore off his multicolored moo moo. He changed the DVD player. His buddies each put on long black wigs and he slipped into a pair of tight sequined underwear. Music came blasting out of the DVD player and on screen, three chocolate women were singing and dancing. Andre and his buddies sang loudly along with the music.

"Stop! In the name of love," Andre called.

"Before you break my heart," his buddies returned, clapping and stepping perfectly along with the tune.

"What is this?" Sue Ellen asked; she'd never heard such great music before.

"Ain't you heard Dina Ross and the Supremiums?"

"Nah, but it's great."

Sue Ellen jumped up and danced in the middle of the three men. Andre grinded her midsection while the other two danced right along with the women on the TV.

"You guys know every dance step."

"Shit yeah. We watch this all the time."

"All the fuckin' time."

The song ended and Sue Ellen stopped. "What happened?"

"Don't worry, pretty thing. Another song is coming."

The music came back on and Sue Ellen leaped into Andre's arms. The music was so exciting. She couldn't contain herself.

"Give it to me. Let me have it!" She bounced on Andre as he leaned into the edge of the bucket seat and slid off his shiny underwear.

"You better slow down! A brother don't like to pull it out."

"Pull nuthin' out! Give it to me!"

"Yeah?"

"Yeah!"

"Yeah?"

"Yeah!"

"Yeah!" they shouted together. And it was done.

Too much to drink and too much damned fun. And a third little baby was all hers. Nine months later, Elie-Dre was born. It was the last child she'd ever give birth to, she vowed. Soon after, Dr. Kurtsworth tied her tubes, supposedly insuring it would never happen again.

NINE

Who the fuck is she talking to now?

"I need help! Someone's gotta help me," *I hear Mommy whine.*

Her bitch friend says back, "You have to go back to Dr. Kurtsworth."

"I can't. He won't do it. He says it's too late to abort."

"Too late?"

"Yes, too late."

That's right, Momma. You ain't gettin' rid of me. You just can't fuck with Super Fetus, Biiiaccch!

"Chrissy, what did you do that time? I know you were broke and didn't use no kinda fancy doctor."

"Honey, you don't want to go to him."

"I have to. I have to get rid of this…this thing in me. I have to! What is his name?"

"His name is Dr. Aburamatoosi. He says he's legit and all, but…"

"Then give me his number."

"But, Sue Ellen."

"His number!"

"He doesn't work out of an office. He has this dungeon. It's awful."

"I said give me the number, Chrissy."

"The guy is creepy. He has this slicked-back, greasy hair that's like, half bald. And his face is all full of pockmarks."

"Chrissy. The number."

"But, Sue Ellen, it still stings when I pee."

"I don't care. I need this thing out of me!"

Keep dreaming, Mommy. Keep dreaming.

❧

Was I napping? Where the hell are we now?

"Sue Ellen, I'm going to run an IV with some medicine," *I hear this guy with a cab-driver accent say,* "it's going to induce your labor. It's the best way at this point to get this taken care of for you."

"I don't care what you have to do, Dr. Aburamatoosi. And I don't care how you have to do it or what it takes. If it hurts it hurts. Just get this thing out of me."

Yeah, well, fuck you too, Mommy.

"Very good, Miss Sue Ellen. I will be taking care of this for you. I will be back when the Pitocin is kicking in."

Okay, another sneaky doctor thinks he can take out Super Fetus. Nuh uh. Not gonna happen.

I'll wait.

❧

Jesus freakin Christ! What is that? It's like an earthquake hit. Not a fuckin' thing to grab hold of. Freakin' bumping around. Something is twisting me and shaking me, tossing me about like I was stuck in a goddamn blender or something.

"Oh, Jesus, Doctor. It really hurts!"

Yeah, Mommy. Finally, we agree on something.

"Just relax, Miss Sue Ellen. It's just a contraction. Breathe in and out. Short quick breaths. You'll be okay."

"It fucking hurts!"

It fucking hurts!

"My fucking back!"

My fucking head!

"Jesus Christ, Doctor, help me!"

Jesus Christ, Doc. Knock it the fuck off!

"Okay, now, Miss Sue Ellen. I know it is much pain, but if you hang in there, you will be getting through this. Trust me."

"It hurts! Get me some morphine!"

"Trust me, Sue Ellen. I could give you something for the pain, but that will only prolong the inevitable. You won't be able to push if you're doped up."

Whoa! It's settling down.

"Okay. Okay." *Mommy is breathing in and out like she'd just run a marathon.*

"Good. You've made it through the contraction. You're going to be fine, Sue Ellen."

Finally. A break. Those things are too much. Oh, man. Here it comes again.

"Oh God! Oh Jesus."

"This is good, Sue Ellen. Just relax. The contractions are very close together. You are going to deliver soon."

"GET THIS THING OUT OF ME!"

"I'm working on it, Sue Ellen. Work with me, not against me."

"AHHHHH! It hurts."

What is that fuckhead fraud of a doctor trying now? Get those fucking things away from my head, Doc! Don't make me show you what I did to the last guy who tried that!

"Okay, Sue Ellen. I feel the head. I've got it."

Come here, fuckhead!

"Oh no!" *The doctor yells. He thought he had me, but I've got him.* "It's so strong!"

"Doctor! Get it out of me!"

"I...I...I can't. It...it...it, it's pulling me in."

Come 'ere, Doc! ARRRRGH!

"It's biting my hand! STOP!"

"Get it out of me, doctor! Please!"

"I can't! Help me! It's pulling me in."

"Doctor! It hurts!"

ARRRRGH!

"Oh, my. AHHHH!"

Got you! How many times do I have to tell these fuckin' people, you do not fuck with Super Fetus!

TEN

≈

Sue Ellen sat in the bathtub, watching and yet trying to ignore the water as it turned from clear to red. Was it her blood? Or Dr. Aburamatoosi's? Or the blood of the thing growing inside of her? The stubborn thing that absolutely refused to die.

"Why is this happening to me?" she cried to the sky.

It was just that: a thing. It was not a baby. It was not human. It was growing inside of her, but it was *not* her baby.

"What the fuck are you?" she screamed at her stomach. The thing punched her back in answer. "You hear every word I say, don't you?" Again, a punch to her gut affirmed it.

The kids were at school. Cleve was at work. She was alone. Alone with *It*.

Sue Ellen lay all the way back in the tub and drifted back to a night at The Lucky Duck. It was her lucky night all right.

Sure it was.

It was the night *It* was conceived. One lucky night at The Lucky Duck.

"Make it a double!" she remembered telling Hank, the peach-fuzzed bartender there. He was such a pretty kid. Too pretty to be tending bar in that dump.

Sue Ellen was mad—mad at Cleve for being such a shit. That's when *He* walked in. Sure, she'd had one-night stands before, and even been in love before. But this was different.

When *He* walked into The Lucky Duck, Sue Ellen was entranced.

He was the strangest looking man she'd ever seen. *He* didn't exactly look like anything. *He* had no face. And yet his face was perfect. *He* seemed to have a strong body beneath the long, dark trench coat, and yet his shoulders had no curves, his legs, his hips, his ass, they weren't quite there.

He seemed to float towards her. *He* whispered something in her ear, yet *He* didn't speak. *He* asked her to leave, and she followed.

He took her to a four star hotel, and yet they were in the back of Cleve's pickup. *He* was tender, gentle and loving, all while fucking the hell out of her until her insides were raw.

What was *He*?

Just at the moment of truth, just seconds before the warm fluids filled her insides, *He* whispered in her ear.

"You will have my baby."

She laughed, as if higher than a Rasta man after huffin' down a Philly blunt. "I don't think so, buddy."

But *He* seemed cocksure.

"You will have my baby."

"Honey, my tubes have been tied. My eggs are dried and there ain't shit comin' out of this hole, 'cept for pee. Okay?"

"You will have my baby."

She laughed. Then pushed him away.

"Jesus fuck!" Sue Ellen screamed, jumping up from the tub. "What the fuck was he?"

Another punch to the gut coming from inside herself.

"Stop it! Leave me alone."

No, Mommy! You leave me alone!

Sue Ellen looked at her belly. Was she hearing things? Had she finally lost her mind?

"You are not human."

⌀

I think Mommy wants me out of here. She just keeps trying to hurt me. I am not leaving. Imagine what that bitch'll do if I come out.
Not a chance. I ain't leaving.

⌀

Sue Ellen stood up in the tub and ran for the door. She ignored the pool of dripping water and blood that followed her, not bothering to get a towel. She was on her way to get something more important than a towel.

⌀

What'd you say, Mommy?
"If those fucking doctors can't take care of this, I'll take care of this myself!"
Holy fuck! Ouch! That fucking hurts, Mommy. Stop!

⌀

Sue Ellen rammed the unraveled coat hanger right up her sore twat. It hurt. But she didn't care anymore. She had to end this. The thing inside her needed to die, and it needed to die now. She could feel the vile thing trembling inside of her.

⌀

Ow, oh, ee, ah! Fuck, stop. Stop. Stop that. Damn it, Mommy, that hurts. Stop poking at me. You're poking holes in my tummy. Enough. Stop it.

That crazy bitch just won't stop hackin' at me and hackin' at me, puncturing hole after hole in my soft pink skin. I can't hold her off.

The pain was excruciating! But it didn't matter. Sue Ellen kept ramming the coat hanger in, then yanking it out, then ramming it back up again.

Soon, she was beyond pain. She didn't feel a thing. The hanger went in and out and in and out with more and more red gunk on it each time.

The trembling inside her increased to a mad rumble.

That's it, Mommy. I am outta here. I am tearing her pussy wide fucking open so I can get the fuck out of here.

Errrrrr! Yes! Freedom. So what if I have a leg missing, half a hand, holes and cuts all over me and a shriveled up head? I still have a mouth and I still have an ass.

Here I am, Mommy. Feed me. Clothe me. Change my shitty diapers, you bitch!

ABOUT THE AUTHOR

At times disturbing and bleak, others raunchy and comical, Adam Pepper's work is known for a unique blend of suspense, horror and speculative fiction. MEMORIA, Adam's debut novel immediately attracted a devoted following, cracking the SHOCKLINES Bestsellers and reaching number one on the Dark Delicacies Best Seller list. His quick-hitting short work has appeared in genre magazines including THE BEST OF HORRORFIND, VOL. 2, SPACE & TIME and the acclaimed four-author collection WAITING FOR OCTOBER which also featured the work of Jeffrey Thomas, Jeff Strand and Sarah Pinborough. Adam's nonfiction credits span from NEW WOMAN MAGAZINE to The Journal News. Adam heads up the New York City Chapter of the Horror Writers Association. Learn more about Adam at www.AdamPepper.com.

Bizarro books

CATALOG — SPRING 2009

Bizarro Books publishes under the following imprints:

www.rawdogscreamingpress.com

www.eraserheadpress.com

www.afterbirthbooks.com

www.swallowdownpress.com

For all your Bizarro needs visit:

WWW.BIZARROCENTRAL.COM

Introduce yourselves to the bizarro genre and all of its authors with the Bizarro Starter Kit series. Each volume features short novels and short stories by ten of the leading bizarro authors, designed to give you a perfect sampling of the genre for only $5 plus shipping.

BB-0X1
"The Bizarro Starter Kit" (Orange)

Featuring D. Harlan Wilson, Carlton Mellick III, Jeremy Robert Johnson, Kevin L Donihe, Gina Ranalli, Andre Duza, Vincent W. Sakowski, Steve Beard, John Edward Lawson, and Bruce Taylor.

236 pages $5

BB-0X2
"The Bizarro Starter Kit" (Blue)

Featuring Ray Fracalossy, Jeremy C. Shipp, Jordan Krall, Mykle Hansen, Andersen Prunty, Eckhard Gerdes, Bradley Sands, Steve Aylett, Christian TeBordo, and Tony Rauch.

244 pages $5

BB-001 **"The Kafka Effekt" D. Harlan Wilson -** A collection of forty-four irreal short stories loosely written in the vein of Franz Kafka, with more than a pinch of William S. Burroughs sprinkled on top. **211 pages $14**

BB-002 **"Satan Burger" Carlton Mellick III -** The cult novel that put Carlton Mellick III on the map ... Six punks get jobs at a fast food restaurant owned by the devil in a city violently overpopulated by surreal alien cultures. **236 pages $14**

BB-003 **"Some Things Are Better Left Unplugged" Vincent Sakwoski -** Join The Man and his Nemesis, the obese tabby, for a nightmare roller coaster ride into this postmodern fantasy. **152 pages $10**

BB-004 **"Shall We Gather At the Garden?" Kevin L Donihe -** Donihe's Debut novel. Midgets take over the world, The Church of Lionel Richie vs. The Church of the Byrds, plant porn and more! **244 pages $14**

BB-005 **"Razor Wire Pubic Hair" Carlton Mellick III -** A genderless humandildo is purchased by a razor dominatrix and brought into her nightmarish world of bizarre sex and mutilation. **176 pages $11**

BB-006 **"Stranger on the Loose" D. Harlan Wilson -** The fiction of Wilson's 2nd collection is planted in the soil of normalcy, but what grows out of that soil is a dark, witty, otherworldly jungle... **228 pages $14**

BB-007 **"The Baby Jesus Butt Plug" Carlton Mellick III -** Using clones of the Baby Jesus for anal sex will be the hip sex fetish of the future. **92 pages $10**

BB-008 **"Fishfleshed" Carlton Mellick III -** The world of the past is an illogical flatland lacking in dimension and color, a sick-scape of crispy squid people wandering the desert for no apparent reason. **260 pages $14**

BB-009 **"Dead Bitch Army" Andre Duza** - Step into a world filled with racist teenagers, cannibals, 100 warped Uncle Sams, automobiles with razor-sharp teeth, living graffiti, and a pissed-off zombie bitch out for revenge. **344 pages $16**

BB-010 **"The Menstruating Mall" Carlton Mellick III** - "The Breakfast Club meets Chopping Mall as directed by David Lynch." - Brian Keene **212 pages $12**

BB-011 **"Angel Dust Apocalypse" Jeremy Robert Johnson** - Meth-heads, man-made monsters, and murderous Neo-Nazis. "Seriously amazing short stories..." - Chuck Palahniuk, author of Fight Club **184 pages $11**

BB-012 **"Ocean of Lard" Kevin L Donihe / Carlton Mellick III** - A parody of those old Choose Your Own Adventure kid's books about some very odd pirates sailing on a sea made of animal fat. **176 pages $12**

   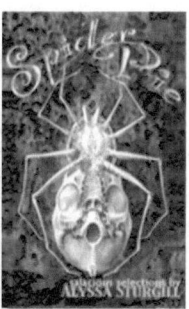

BB-013 **"Last Burn in Hell" John Edward Lawson** - From his lurid angst-affair with a lesbian music diva to his ascendance as unlikely pop icon the one constant for Kenrick Brimley, official state prison gigolo, is he's got no clue what he's doing. **172 pages $14**

BB-014 **"Tangerinephant" Kevin Dole 2** - TV-obsessed aliens have abducted Michael Tangerinephant in this bizarro combination of science fiction, satire, and surrealism. **164 pages $11**

BB-015 **"Foop!" Chris Genoa** - Strange happenings are going on at Dactyl, Inc, the world's first and only time travel tourism company.

"A surreal pie in the face!" - Christopher Moore **300 pages $14**

BB-016 **"Spider Pie" Alyssa Sturgill** - A one-way trip down a rabbit hole inhabited by sexual deviants and friendly monsters, fairytale beginnings and hideous endings. **104 pages $11**

BB-017 "The Unauthorized Woman" Efrem Emerson - Enter the world of the inner freak, a landscape populated by the pre-dead and morticioners, by cockroaches and 300-lb robots. **104 pages $11**

BB-018 "Fugue XXIX" Forrest Aguirre - Tales from the fringe of speculative literary fiction where innovative minds dream up the future's uncharted territories while mining forgotten treasures of the past. **220 pages $16**

BB-019 "Pocket Full of Loose Razorblades" John Edward Lawson - A collection of dark bizarro stories. From a giant rectum to a foot-fungus factory to a girl with a biforked tongue. **190 pages $13**

BB-020 "Punk Land" Carlton Mellick III - In the punk version of Heaven, the anarchist utopia is threatened by corporate fascism and only Goblin, Mortician's sperm, and a blue-mohawked female assassin named Shark Girl can stop them. **284 pages $15**

BB-021 "Pseudo-City" D. Harlan Wilson - Pseudo-City exposes what waits in the bathroom stall, under the manhole cover and in the corporate boardroom, all in a way that can only be described as mind-bogglingly irreal. **220 pages $16**

BB-022 "Kafka's Uncle and Other Strange Tales" Bruce Taylor - Anslenot and his giant tarantula (tormentor? fri-end?) wander a desecrated world in this novel and collection of stories from Mr. Magic Realism Himself. **348 pages $17**

BB-023 "Sex and Death In Television Town" Carlton Mellick III - In the old west, a gang of hermaphrodite gunslingers take refuge from a demon plague in Telos: a town where its citizens have televisions instead of heads. **184 pages $12**

BB-024 "It Came From Below The Belt" Bradley Sands - What can Grover Goldstein do when his severed, sentient penis forces him to return to high school and help it win the presidential election? **204 pages $13**

BB-025 **"Sick: An Anthology of Illness" John Lawson, editor** - These Sick stories are horrendous and hilarious dissections of creative minds on the scalpel's edge. **296 pages $16**

BB-026 **"Tempting Disaster" John Lawson, editor** - A shocking and alluring anthology from the fringe that examines our culture's obsession with taboos. **260 pages $16**

BB-027 **"Siren Promised" Jeremy Robert Johnson** - Nominated for the Bram Stoker Award. A potent mix of bad drugs, bad dreams, brutal bad guys, and surreal/incredible art by Alan M. Clark. **190 pages $13**

BB-028 **"Chemical Gardens" Gina Ranalli** - Ro and punk band Green is the Enemy find Kreepkins, a surfer-dude warlock, a vengeful demon, and a Metal Priestess in their way as they try to escape an underground nightmare. **188 pages $13**

BB-029 **"Jesus Freaks" Andre Duza** - For God so loved the world that he gave his only two begotten sons… and a few million zombies. **400 pages $16**

BB-030 **"Grape City" Kevin L. Donihe** - More Donihe-style comedic bizarro about a demon named Charles who is forced to work a minimum wage job on Earth after Hell goes out of business. **108 pages $10**

BB-031 **"Sea of the Patchwork Cats" Carlton Mellick III** - A quiet dreamlike tale set in the ashes of the human race. For Mellick enthusiasts who also adore The Twilight Zone. **112 pages $10**

BB-032 **"Extinction Journals" Jeremy Robert Johnson** - An uncanny voyage across a newly nuclear America where one man must confront the problems associated with loneliness, insane dieties, radiation, love, and an ever-evolving cockroach suit with a mind of its own. **104 pages $10**

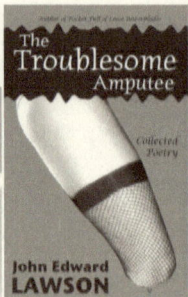

BB-033 "Meat Puppet Cabaret" Steve Beard - At last! The secret connection between Jack the Ripper and Princess Diana's death revealed! **240 pages $16 / $30**

BB-034 "The Greatest Fucking Moment in Sports" Kevin L. Donihe - In the tradition of the surreal anti-sitcom Get A Life comes a tale of triumph and agape love from the master of comedic bizarro. **108 pages $10**

BB-035 "The Troublesome Amputee" John Edward Lawson - Disturbing verse from a man who truly believes nothing is sacred and intends to prove it. **104 pages $9**

BB-036 "Deity" Vic Mudd - God (who doesn't like to be called "God") comes down to a typical, suburban, Ohio family for a little vacation—but it doesn't turn out to be as relaxing as He had hoped it would be... **168 pages $12**

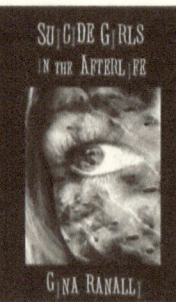

BB-037 "The Haunted Vagina" Carlton Mellick III - It's difficult to love a woman whose vagina is a gateway to the world of the dead. **132 pages $10**

BB-038 "Tales from the Vinegar Wasteland" Ray Fracalossy - Witness: a man is slowly losing his face, a neighbor who periodically screams out for no apparent reason, and a house with a room that doesn't actually exist. **240 pages $14**

BB-039 "Suicide Girls in the Afterlife" Gina Ranalli - After Pogue commits suicide, she unexpectedly finds herself an unwilling "guest" at a hotel in the Afterlife, where she meets a group of bizarre characters, including a goth Satan, a hippie Jesus, and an alien-human hybrid. **100 pages $9**

BB-040 "And Your Point Is?" Steve Aylett - In this follow-up to LINT multiple authors provide critical commentary and essays about Jeff Lint's mind-bending literature. **104 pages $11**

BB-041 "Not Quite One of the Boys" Vincent Sakowski - While drug-dealer Maxi drinks with Dante in purgatory, God and Satan play a little tri-level chess and do a little bargaining over his business partner, Vinnie, who is still left on earth. **220 pages $14**

BB-042 "Teeth and Tongue Landscape" Carlton Mellick III - On a planet made out of meat, a socially-obsessive monophobic man tries to find his place amongst the strange creatures and communities that he comes across. **110 pages $10**

BB-043 "War Slut" Carlton Mellick III - Part "1984," part "Waiting for Godot," and part action horror video game adaptation of John Carpenter's "The Thing." **116 pages $10**

BB-044 "All Encompassing Trip" Nicole Del Sesto - In a world where coffee is no longer available, the only television shows are reality TV re-runs, and the animals are talking back, Nikki, Amber and a singing Coyote in a do-rag are out to restore the light **308 pages $15**

BB-045 "Dr. Identity" D. Harlan Wilson - Follow the Dystopian Duo on a killing spree of epic proportions through the irreal postcapitalist city of Bliptown where time ticks sideways, artificial Bug-Eyed Monsters punish citizens for consumer-capitalist lethargy, and ultraviolence is as essential as a daily multivitamin. **208 pages $15**

BB-046 "The Million-Year Centipede" Eckhard Gerdes - Wakelin, frontman for 'The Hinge,' wrote a poem so prophetic that to ignore it dooms a person to drown in blood. **130 pages $12**

BB-047 "Sausagey Santa" Carlton Mellick III - A bizarro Christmas tale featuring Santa as a piratey mutant with a body made of sausages. 124 pages $10

BB-048 "Misadventures in a Thumbnail Universe" Vincent Sakowski - Dive deep into the surreal and satirical realms of neo-classical Blender Fiction, filled with television shoes and flesh-filled skies. **120 pages $10**

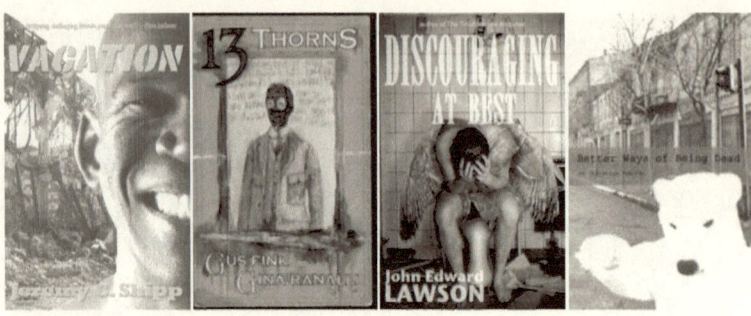

BB-049 **"Vacation" Jeremy C. Shipp** - Blueblood Bernard Johnson leaved his boring life behind to go on The Vacation, a year-long corporate sponsored odyssey. But instead of seeing the world, Bernard is captured by terrorists, becomes a key figure in secret drug wars, and, worse, doesn't once miss his secure American Dream.   **160 pages $14**

BB-051 **"13 Thorns" Gina Ranalli** - Thirteen tales of twisted, bizarro horror. **240 pages $13**

BB-050 **"Discouraging at Best" John Edward Lawson** - A collection where the absurdity of the mundane expands exponentially creating a tidal wave that sweeps reason away. For those who enjoy satire, bizarro, or a good old-fashioned slap to the senses. **208 pages $15**

BB-052 **"Better Ways of Being Dead" Christian TeBordo** - In this class, the students have to keep one palm down on the table at all times, and listen to lectures about a panda who speaks Chinese. **216 pages $14**

BB-053 **"Ballad of a Slow Poisoner" Andrew Goldfarb** Millford Mutterwurst sat down on a Tuesday to take his afternoon tea, and made the unpleasant discovery that his elbows were becoming flatter. **128 pages $10**

BB-054 **"Wall of Kiss" Gina Ranalli** - A woman... A wall... Sometimes love blooms in the strangest of places. **108 pages $9**

BB-055 **"HELP! A Bear is Eating Me" Mykle Hansen** - The bizarro, heartwarming, magical tale of poor planning, hubris and severe blood loss... **150 pages $11**

BB-056 **"Piecemeal June" Jordan Krall** - A man falls in love with a living sex doll, but with love comes danger when her creator comes after her with crab-squid assassins. **90 pages $9**

BB-057 **"Laredo" Tony Rauch** - Dreamlike, surreal stories by Tony Rauch. **180 pages $12**

BB-058 **"The Overwhelming Urge" Andersen Prunty** - A collection of bizarro tales by Andersen Prunty. **150 pages $11**

BB-059 **"Adolf in Wonderland" Carlton Mellick III** - A dreamlike adventure that takes a young descendant of Adolf Hitler's design and sends him down the rabbit hole into a world of imperfection and disorder. **180 pages $11**

BB-060 **"Super Cell Anemia" Duncan B. Barlow** - "Unrelentingly bizarre and mysterious, unsettling in all the right ways..." - Brian Evenson. **180 pages $12**

BB-061 **"Ultra Fuckers" Carlton Mellick III** - Absurdist suburban horror about a couple who enter an upper middle class gated community but can't find their way out. **108 pages $9**

BB-062 **"House of Houses" Kevin L. Donihe** - An odd man wants to marry his house. Unfortunately, all of the houses in the world collapse at the same time in the Great House Holocaust. Now he must travel to House Heaven to find his departed fiancee. **172 pages $11**

BB-063 **"Necro Sex Machine" Andre Duza** - The Dead Bicth returns in this follow-up to the bizarro zombie epic Dead Bitch Army. **400 pages $16**

BB-064 **"Squid Pulp Blues" Jordan Krall** - In these three bizarro-noir novellas, the reader is thrown into a world of murderers, drugs made from squid parts, deformed gun-toting veterans, and a mischievous apocalyptic donkey. **204 pages $12**

BB-065 **"Jack and Mr. Grin" Andersen Prunty** - "When Mr. Grin calls you can hear a smile in his voice. Not a warm and friendly smile, but the kind that seizes your spine in fear. You don't need to pay your phone bill to hear it. That smile is in every line of Prunty's prose." - Tom Bradley. **208 pages $12**

BB-066 **"Cybernetrix" Carlton Mellick III** - What would you do if your normal everyday world was slowly mutating into the video game world from Tron? **212 pages $12**

BB-067 **"Lemur" Tom Bradley** - Spencer Sproul is a would-be serial-killing bus boy who can't manage to murder, injure, or even scare anybody. However, there are other ways to do damage to far more people and do it legally... **120 pages $12**

BB-068 **"Cocoon of Terror" Jason Earls** - Decapitated corpses...a sculpture of terror...Zelian's masterpiece, his Cocoon of Terror, will trigger a supernatural disaster for everyone on Earth. **196 pages $14**

BB-069 **"Mother Puncher" Gina Ranalli** - The world has become tragically over-populated and now the government strongly opposes procreation. Ed is employed by the government as a mother-puncher. He doesn't relish his job, but he knows it has to be done and he knows he's the best one to do it. **120 pages $9**

BB-070 **"My Landlady the Lobotomist" Eckhard Gerdes** - The brains of past tenants line the shelves of my boarding house, soaking in a mysterious elixir. One more slip-up and the landlady might just add my frontal lobe to her collection. **116 pages $12**

BB-071 **"CPR for Dummies" Mickey Z.** - This hilarious freakshow at the world's end is the fragmented, sobering debut novel by acclaimed nonfiction author Mickey Z. **216 pages $14**

BB-072 **"Zerostrata" Andersen Prunty** - Hansel Nothing lives in a tree house, suffers from memory loss, has a very eccentric family, and falls in love with a woman who runs naked through the woods every night. **144 pages $11**

BB-073 **"The Egg Man" Carlton Mellick III** - It is a world where humans reproduce like insects. Children are the property of corporations, and having an enormous ten-foot brain implanted into your skull is a grotesque sexual fetish. Mellick's industrial urban dystopia is one of his darkest and grittiest to date. **184 pages $11**

BB-074 **"Shark Hunting in Paradise Garden" Cameron Pierce** - A group of strange humanoid religious fanatics travel back in time to the Garden of Eden to discover it is invested with hundreds of giant flying maneating sharks. **150 pages $10**

BB-075 **"Apeshit" Carlton Mellick III** - Friday the 13th meets Visitor Q. Six hipster teens go to a cabin in the woods inhabited by a deformed killer. An incredibly fucked-up parody of B-horror movies with a bizarro slant. **192 pages $12**

BB-076 **"Rampaging Fuckers of Everything on the Crazy Shitting Planet of the Vomit At smosphere" Mykle Hansen** - 3 bizarro satires. Monster Cocks, Journey to the Center of Agnes Cuddlebottom, and Crazy Shitting Planet. **228 pages $12**

BB-077 **"The Kissing Bug" Daniel Scott Buck** - In the tradition of Roald Dahl, Tim Burton, and Edward Gorey, comes this bizarro anti-war children's story about a bohemian conenose kissing bug who falls in love with a human woman. **116 pages $10**

BB-078 **"MachoPoni" Lotus Rose** - It's My Little Pony... *Bizarro* style! A long time ago Poniworld was split in two. On one side of the Jagged Line is the Pastel Kingdom, a magical land of music, parties, and positivity. On the other side of the Jagged Line is Dark Kingdom inhabited by an army of undead ponies. **148 pages $11**

BB-079 **"The Faggiest Vampire" Carlton Mellick III** - A Roald Dahlesque children's story about two faggy vampires who partake in a mustache competition to find out which one is truly the faggiest. **104 pages $10**

BB-080 **"Sky Tongues" Gina Ranalli** - The autobiography of Sky Tongues, the biracial hermaphrodite actress with tongues for fingers. Follow her strange life story as she rises from freak to fame. **204 pages $12**

BB-081 **"Washer Mouth" Kevin L. Donihe** - A washing machine becomes human and pursues his dream of meeting his favorite soap opera star. **244 pages $11**

BB-082 **"Shatnerquake" Jeff Burk** - All of the characters ever played by William Shatner are suddenly sucked into our world. Their mission: hunt down and destroy the real William Shatner. **100 pages $10**

BB-083 **"The Cannibals of Candyland" Carlton Mellick III** - There exists a race of cannibals that are made of candy. They live in an underground world made out of candy. One man has dedicated his life to killing them all. **170 pages $11**

BB-084 **"Slub Glub in the Weird World of the Weeping Willows"** **Andrew Goldfarb** - The charming tale of a blue glob named Slub Glub who helps the weeping willows whose tears are flooding the earth. There are also hyenas, ghosts, and a voodoo priest **100 pages $10**

COMING SOON

"Fistful of Feet" by Jordan Krall
"Ass Goblins of Auschwitz" by Cameron Pierce
"Cursed" by Jeremy C. Shipp
"Warrior Wolf Women of the Wasteland"
by Carlton Mellick III
"The Kobold Wizard's Dildo of Enlightenment +2"
by Carlton Mellick III

ORDER FORM

TITLES	QTY	PRICE	TOTAL

Please make checks and moneyorders payable to ROSE O'KEEFE / BIZARRO BOOKS in U.S. funds only. Please don't send bad checks! Allow 2-6 weeks for delivery. International orders may take longer. If you'd like to pay online via PAYPAL.COM, send payments to publisher@eraserheadpress.com.

SHIPPING: US ORDERS - $2 for the first book, $1 for each additional book. For priority shipping, add an additional $4. INT'L ORDERS - $5 for the first book, $3 for each additional book. Add an additional $5 per book for global priority shipping.

Send payment to:

BIZARRO BOOKS
 C/O Rose O'Keefe
 205 NE Bryant
 Portland, OR 97211

Address	
City	State Zip
Email	Phone